"JEAN LORRAIN" (1855-190
Paul Duval, adopted at the insist
ship-owner, who wanted to prote
disgrace of employment by a poe
dandy, when forced to make a living from his pen after his father died ruined, he became one of the most prolific and highest-paid journalists of the *fin-de-siècle*, and the personification, in his lifestyle as well as his writing, of the Decadent Movement. *Monsieur de Phocas. Astarté* (1901; tr. as *Monsieur de Phocas*), compounded out of numerous short stories, is a kind of retrospective summary of the Decadent world-view, written after he was forced to leave Paris because of health problems occasioned by his use of ether as a stimulant, which did not take long to kill him thereafter. English translations of some of his short stories are contained in *Nightmares of an Ether-Drinker* (Tartarus Press, 2002; reprinted by Snuggly Books, 2016), *The Soul-Drinker and Other Decadent Fantasies* (Snuggly Books, 2016) and *Masks in the Tapestry* (Snuggly Books, 2017).

BRIAN STABLEFORD'S scholarly work includes *New Atlantis: A Narrative History of Scientific Romance* (Wildside Press, 2016), *The Plurality of Imaginary Worlds: The Evolution of French roman scientifique* (Black Coat Press, 2017) and *Tales of Enchantment and Disenchantment: A History of Faerie* (Black Coat Press, 2019). In support of the latter projects he has translated more than a hundred volumes of roman scientifique and more than twenty volumes of contes de fées into English. He has edited *Decadence and Symbolism: A Showcase Anthology* (Snuggly Books, 2018), and is busy translating more Symbolist and Decadent fiction.

SNUGGLY BOOKS

JEAN LORRAIN

PRINCESSES OF DARKNESS
AND OTHER EXOTICA

TRANSLATED AND WITH AN INTRODUCTION BY
BRIAN STABLEFORD

THIS IS A SNUGGLY BOOK

ISBN: 978-1-64525-069-2

CONTENTS

INTRODUCTION

WHEN Jean Lorrain was recruited to the stable of writers assembled by Catulle Mendès to supply *L'Écho de Paris* with material on a weekly basis, in July 1890, he joined in readily with the experimental spirit of that enterprise, exploring various narrative strategies that could be employed in fitting work to slots that varied in length between 1,000 and 2,000 words. The contributions to the paper that he signed with his own name were soon outnumbered by the items that he signed "Raitif de la Bretonne," in honor of the prolifically innovative Nicolas-Edmé Restif de la Bretonne (1734-1806), most of whose publications had appeared without the royal warrant necessary prior to the 1789 Revolution for works to be printed and sold legally.

Restif had spent most of his life before the Revolution compiling an autobiography that, he claimed, would "lay the human heart bare"—an ambition taken up explicitly by numerous later writers, including another of Jean Lorrain's heroes, Charles Baudelaire. Restif imported elements of his autobiography-in-progress into several of his novels, and also produced several items of fiction that pretended to be autobiographical, most notably *Les Nuits de Paris* (8 vols., 1786-92), which chronicled his supposed adventures in urban noctambulism—a work that had a profound influence on Lorrain.

The works to which Lorrain attached the Raitif signature were various, but they included two long series of particular significance. The first, begun in 1891, bore the heading *Une Femme par jour* [A Woman a Day] and consisted of a long series of sarcastic character sketches of alleged female types, often citing specific examples of the supposed types, which employed fictitious names but whose referents were sometimes identifiable. Whether or not the analyses in question really laid the heart of the human female bare is open to question, but they certainly displayed Lorrain's caustic wit and his peculiar attitude to the female of the species, the uneasy paradoxicality of which is extravagantly displayed in such items as "Loreley" and "Princesses de ténébres" [Princesses of Darkness].

The *Femme par jour* series was followed by a much longer one bearing the heading *Pall Mall Semaine* [Pall Mall Week], which allegedly chronicled "Raitif's" social life and nocturnal expeditions in and around Paris. The enigmatic title was probably chosen because Lorrain intended the pieces in question to echo Oscar Wilde's contributions to W. T. Stead's *Pall Mall Gazette*, a significant model for the *Écho de Paris*. Again, the series often employed fictitious names for the characters featured therein, but he did not hesitate to drop real ones whenever it seemed safe or appropriate, and it earned Lorrain more than one slap in the face and more than one lawsuit as he gradually became more brazen and more flagrantly insulting in his sarcastic assaults. When he deserted the *Écho* in 1895 to write for *Le Journal* he took Raitif, the *Pall Mall Semaine* and the associated scandals with him.

From the very beginning, all of Lorrain's contributions to the *Écho* blurred the boundary between fiction and non-fiction. He frequently embedded stories within essays, or situated them within conversation-pieces or embroidered accounts of his various travels. Eventually, almost all of his short stories for *Le Journal* were represented as second-hand narratives supposedly derived from conversations, although the narrative voice to whom the transmission was credited was often given a name that was not "Jean Lorrain"—but Jean Lorrain was, of course, a fictitious person himself, invented by one Paul Duval (1855-1906), allegedly to save his respectable family name from the disgrace of literary association. Lorrain not only wrote but lived a long series of lies, albeit rather uneasily; his fiction and reportage drew relentlessly on supposed memories of his childhood in Normandy as well as his nocturnal adventures in Paris and various locations on the Mediterranean. His work also toyed, indirectly and sometimes teasingly with the homosexual desires that he never managed to repress or embrace wholeheartedly, although he elected briefly to display them flamboyantly when he thought that he had become famous enough to defy the censure of Parisian society.

While it was being managed by Catulle Mendès between 1889 and 1895 the *Écho* stable was a remarkable cauldron of experimentation, as its various contributors tried out all manner of methods for condensing short stories into a straitjacket that rarely exceeded 2,000 words and averaged considerably less. In terms of their fundamental narrative structure, almost all the items thus produced were "*contes cruels*," orientated toward endings that celebrated "the irony of fate" rather than the "happy endings" typical of long fiction—especially the "feuilleton" fiction serialized in the great majority of Parisian newspapers. The "cruelty" of such stories was, however, routinely softened in various ways. Although one of the members of the stable, Jean Reibrach, employed the uncompromising heading *La Vie brutale* [Brutal Life] for his stories, and a few others, notably Octave Mirbeau, also seemed to relish the sadistic aspects of their work, Mendès and his closest associate, Armand Silvestre, preferred to temper the brutality of their fiction by employing an essentially amiable, flippant and teasing irony, usually in the context of the "war of the sexes," contested between men intent on wily serial seduction and women in quest of "true" (i.e. faithful) love.

Mendès, who employed the heading *La Vie serieuse* [Serious Life] for many of his stories, and such headings as *Les Légendes tendres* [Tender Legends] and *Nouveaux contes de jadis* [New Tales of Old] for more exotic ones, was particularly fond of locating his calculatedly immoral apologues within fantasized narratives, and he became the most prolific *fin-de-siècle* author of modern *contes de fées*, pastiches of saintly legends and fantasies set in paradise. Several of his stablemates followed such examples occasionally, but most of them preferred to stick exclusively to naturalistic narratives, and that was the way that the wind of reader demand was blowing; by 1900 such material had been almost entirely purged from the arena of newspaper short fiction, although Mendès stubbornly persisted in his peccadilloes, and a few of his disciples followed his example for a while, even though they were well aware that they were swimming against a forceful tide. Jean Lorrain was one such, although his "tender legends" were easily distinguishable from Mendès' by virtue of their solemn tone; although not entirely lacking in amiability or flippancy, they were usually very earnest and sometimes uncommonly intense. The lighter ones were usually nostalgic, referring back fondly to the love of such stories that had possessed the author in his youth, but even they tended to be embittered, subjecting the innate optimism of stories told to children to a cynical reevaluation. Lorrain's tales of enchantment, unlike Mendès', tended to be *contes cruels* of an insistently harsh stripe, striking a note that was both plangent and calculatedly discordant, although he was sufficiently versatile to indulge a careful piety in such sentimental tales as "Les Niais de Malhantôt" [The Idiots of Malhantôt].

In their original publication in *L'Écho de Paris* and *Le Journal*, Lorrain's occasional fantasies were mingled randomly with a profusion of naturalistic stories, travel articles, critical articles and essays, and such was his method of procedure that those categories often overlapped inventively. Eventually, he separated out what he presumably considered to be the cream of the crop of his legendary *contes* into a volume entitled *Princesses d'ivoire et d'ivresse* (1902). All of the items in that collection have been translated into English, but the translations are distributed in batches over a number of volumes, four items in *Nightmares of an Ether-Drinker* (2002), eight in *The Soul Drinker and Other Decadent Fantasies* (2016) and eleven in *Masks in the Tapestry* (2017). There are, however, a number of related items that appeared in the pages of the two newspapers but were omitted from *Princesses d'ivoire et d'ivresse,* probably because the author considered them marginal, some of them not being stories at all. Most of the items in question are translated in the present volume, in the chronological order of their appearance, thus casting some illumination on the development of the author's ideas and narrative strategies.

The first items in the collection are based on paintings—a source of inspiration that Lorrain had often used for his poems, written purely for art's sake, before the death of his bankrupt father cast him into penury and forced him to make his living by means of his pen, in the only marketplace available to him that offered the possibility of making a living. Basing his fantastic stories on works of art, and forming them as "poems in prose"—sometimes with formal poems incorporated into them—was an apologetic strategy that he often employed to justify swimming against the tide of opinion before he gathered the confidence to oppose that tide defiantly. Mendès and Silvestre often used the same stratagem. Although such allegories as "La Tapisserie d'Eros" [The Tapestry of Eros] (published under the heading "Roses lointaines" [Distant roses]), "Un Primitif" [A Primitive] and "Trois Dames dans l'île" [Three Ladies on the Island] make no such apology, there is a tacit distancing built into their uncompromising cynicism. A similar narrative distance is preserved in "Loreley," one of the author's rare ventures into historical fiction—an arena in which he must have been well aware of his inability to compete with the relentlessly scholarly Marcel Schwob, perhaps the finest writer in the Mendès stable, who set the pace for the rest.

One of his employments of works of art as a source of inspiration was to play a notable role in Lorrain's career, illustrating a particular perversity in his extrapolation of that influence: his discovery of a small exhibition of pastels by a reclusive young artist named Jeanne Jacquemin, as described in the strange essay for which the present collection is titled. He dedicated several stories to her and heaped praise upon her in his critical writings, including the essay "Trois têtes" [Three Heads] (*L'Écho de Paris* 5 May 1893), for which she was initially grateful, although that gratitude must have been badly soured by the nature of the "praise" that he incorporated into his study of "Princesses de ténèbres."

There can be no doubt that in coupling Jeanne Jacquemin with another of his protégées, Rachilde, Lorrain imagined that he was being entirely complimentary, and it does not seem to have occurred to him that, although the ever-controversial Rachilde undoubtedly relished being categorized as one of the "elect of Satan," the mystically-inclined Jeanne Jacquemin might not. Five years later, Jacquemin sued Lorrain for defamation of character after he employed a thinly disguised representation of her in "Victime," (1903; tr. as "Victim" in the 2019 collection *Fards and Poisons*), part of a story-series entitled *Femmes* in *Le Journal* that echoed his pseudonymous *Écho* series *Une Femme par jour*. That story is, in fact, fairly innocuous, but it undoubtedly awoke sore memories of "Les Princesses de ténèbres" in its exemplar, and proved to be the last straw in stimulating her rancor. The lawsuit was successful and she was awarded unreasonably high damages, although she eventually relented in her pursuit and allowed the judgment to be overturned on appeal.

The displacement strategy employed in drawing inspiration from works of art is further complicated in "Le Prince Frog" [The Frog Prince], which features a secondary embedding in an eccentric conversation piece, making it one of the oddest of Lorrain's *contes*. A similar second layer is employed in the article that was headed—perhaps by the paper's editor rather than the author, given that it also carries the title "Ilse"—"Fairy Land" (in English), which is a commentary on a novel signed "Ossit," by another of Lorrain's female acquaintances, albeit one who did not require his promotion, although it is ironically significant that she has now been almost completely forgotten, primarily remembered as the subject of a scurrilous anecdote invented and put about by Robert de Montesquiou, a flamboyant homosexual whom Lorrain envied and loathed even while employing him as a role model.

The straightforward legendary fantasies that Lorrain began to publish in 1892, devoid of any kind of apologetic frame, were mostly collected in *Princesses d'ivoire et d'ivresse*, but one of the earliest, "Tiphaine," was omitted from that collection, for reasons that are not obvious, although it is a transfiguration of the famous tale of Raymond of Lusignan and the lamia Melusine, which he had already adapted in "Melusine" (*L'Écho de Paris* 18 November 1892; tr. in *Masks in the Tapestry*). "Tiphaine" transplanted the legend to the region of northern France where Lorrain was born; he had briefly cited another transplantation of the same tale in "Contes de l'oie" [Goose Tales] (*L'Écho des Paris* 9 January 1891; reprinted in a nostalgic series of stories published in *Le Journal* in 1903, translated in *Monsieur de Bougrelon and Other Stories*, 2020). The similarly straightforward "Le Champ des pensées" [The Field of Pansies] and "La Bague d'or" [The Gold Ring] might have been omitted from *Princesses d'ivoire et d'ivresse* because they did not seem to their author to be strong enough to warrant inclusion, but they are not significantly weaker than many of the stories that he did include.

Lorrain always seemed more comfortable when framing his fantasies in various ways, so as to deflect any suspicion that he might be taking them too seriously, and his characterization of substitute narrators, such as the old crone of the "Petit contes d'autumne" [Little Tales of Autumn] emphasizes that attitude, which is reproduced in almost all of his many contemporary hallucinatory fantasies, of which a sample is included herein in "La Main gantée" [The Gloved Hand]. Although it is not affiliated to the set of his *contes d'un buveur d'éther* [Tales of an Ether-Drinker] the story in question is very similar to them in spirit, and appears to be loosely based on a similar personal experience, suggesting that the after-effects of his use of ether persisted for some time after he moved out of his "haunted house" in the Rue de Courty, where he has employed the stimulant to keep him awake while he first began to produce copy in profusion for various newspapers.

It is significant that the only story included in the present collection in which the author features quite explicitly as a presence, "Lui!" [Him!], refers back to an auspicious occasion when Lorrain persuaded Marcel Schwob—who was then assisting Oscar Wilde to render *Salomé* into French because it could not be staged in London—to bring the author to dinner at his house in Auteuil (he also invited Anatole France, in order to add further prestige to the company). It is to Wilde that he attributes the mildly blasphemous anecdote, clearly designed for an audience very different from the dedicatee of "Les Niais de Malhantôt." The story cites *The Picture of Dorian Gray* (1890) in order to indicate the reference of its title, but Lorrain probably considered Wilde's masterpiece to be *A House of Pomegranates* (1891), and it is the spirit of that collection of "fairy stories" that he attempted to emulate in his own excursions into "Fairy Land."

Although the present collection is something of a Rabelaisian salmagundi, and contains nothing to match the brilliance of "Conte pour faire peur" [A Tale to Terrify] (*L'Écho de Paris* 31 December 1893 & 1 January 1894; reprinted as a booklet entitled *La Mandragore* [The Mandrake]) or "Sainte Hilde de Courlande" (*Le*

Journal 24 December 1897; reprinted as "La Princesse sous verre" [The Princess under Glass]), both featured in *The Soul Drinker and Other Decadent Fantasies*, its contents partake in the same meticulously perverse point of view and exhibit the same unique literary hallmark; the collection thus performs a useful function in completing an eccentric set with the relevant sections of the earlier volumes of translations.

—Brian Stableford, November 2020.

PRINCESSES OF DARKNESS
AND OTHER EXOTICA

KING COPHETUA[1]

(*L'Écho de Paris*, 22 August 1892; reprinted in *Le Journal* 28 March 1896 as "Le Conte du Mendiant" [The Beggar's Tale])

For Jacques Marie, after Burne-Jones

INTO the finest room in his palace, King Cophetua has led the beggar-maid by the hand; there, between the tall columns of onyx and porphyry, the polish of which is darkened and magnified by the shiny floor-tiles, he makes her climb on to the platform of the throne, which is surrounded by a golden gallery like the perforated grille of a cathedral choir, and gently, with prayerful eyes and gestures of tender pity, he sits her down there.

---

1 Cophetua is the name attributed to a fictitious king in a Medieval ballad, preserved in several anthologies, generally known in English as "The King and the Beggar-Maid": an account of unlikely love at first sight, which ends happily. Shakespeare referenced it several times, and Tennyson produced a version of it that was the inspiration for a famous painting by Edward Burne-Jones exhibited in 1884, on which Lorrain's skeptical piece is based, via a copy made by a French illustrator (credited in the dedication) in a book of traditional tales. Little seems to be recorded about the illustrator in question, save that he was born in 1868.

And the beggar-maid obeys him; resigned and mute in her humble gray dress with holes, she has let herself fall on the cushions of the throne and has crossed the bloodstained ivory of her poor bare feet; her unkempt chestnut-brown hair frames a forehead so divinely calm and two large bright eyes so profoundly pure that none of the courtiers and noble dignitaries is astonished by their seigneur's choice.

O magical power of ineffable beauty, O sure charm, stronger than the ambition and pride of the great, of a forgiving visage formed by suffering and tenderness!

She had only needed to appear at the bend in the bleak and sunlit road, her bare feet in the dust and the wind of the hedges in her rags to enter like the thrust of a knife into the king's heart; she was so sad and so weary, standing in the crushing heat of the day, with the monotonous yellow expanse of the wheat behind her, so weary and yet so courageous, retaining such pride in her outstretched hand, requesting alms . . .

The surprised king had thought he saw appearing before him the errant soul of the people, the suffering of the petty and the humble, but the soul of the people remaining noble, which begs but does not sell itself. Then too, Cophetua had never seen that blue flame of a vigilant and sad gaze in the eyes of any woman, neither in those of the prostitutes of the city nor the caressant and neglectful eyes of the ladies of his court. Bowing down before the vagabond, his forehead low, he had taken her hand and, sketching the gesture of placing a crown on the head of the humiliated woman, he had cried: "This one shall be my queen; I give my word on that to the gentle Seigneur Eros." And all the servants, lieges and vassals of the throne had lowered their heads, acquiescing with that choice, understanding his amour.

And now, in the silence and the solitude of the vast cool hall, the king is sitting facing the beggar-maid and is gazing ardently, rapt in mute contemplation, motionless, as if in prayer, at the humble pauperess collapsed on the throne, whose great pure eyes, infinitely sad, are already following, through the open window, the ribbon of the road snaking through the wheat beneath the hot sky.

Oh, those melancholy eyes, which are already plunging regretfully into the past! Blinded by joy and visionary amour, Cophetua does not see them; seated, his knee bent, facing the platform where the lady of his desires is dreaming languidly, he drinks her avidly with his gaze, choking tumultuous words between his lips and stammering voicelessly, his throat tight, letting his crown dangle in his inert hands, more reminiscent of a statue in his armor of nielloed steel than a living being.

Above his head, a symbol of his fervent hope, a verdant branch extends through the perforated golden enclosure of the throne.

The warrior king gazes at the pauperess, while the amazed beggar-maid, already a queen, gazes into the distance, elsewhere. Oh, eternal and cruel scorn, irony of the benefits of Eros!

Leaning on the rail of the upper gallery, high above the friezes of the deserted hall, two musician pages are singing, two pages dangerous to childish and perverse beauty, reminiscent of two girls beneath their heavy and curly tresses; and the vast hall fills mutedly with their exceedingly tender, passionate and sweet love song.

Young today, old tomorrow!
Raise your eyes, and in your hand
Placing your forehead, listen and weep!
Love today; soon the hour will come
When those who say to you: "always,"
Will no longer think about you.
Skin ashen, neglected in your turn,
Barefoot, you will see the Amours alarmed.
Deliver your mouth to the amorous mouth
Of your lover; life is hollow,
Amour alone fills it, whether blond, red- or
    brown-haired,
And everyone's desire soon ends.

In the orchard the grass is tall and florid,
Under the apple trees, since he implores you, allow
Your sweet seigneur to lie down and swoon beside you;
See, his breath is burning; let the same tender emotion
Make you palpitate together, heart to heart.
Like an enormous flower between the aspens.
The ardent moon and opportune midnight
Have sounded for you the hour of fevers;
Allow your lips to peck and bite,
Everyone's desire soon fades away.

Soon will come the hour when, in the wild grass,
Leaves will fall, and sweet words,
Oaths and tender confessions,
Like the rosebuds in your hair
Beside your pink ear.

24

Soon will come the hour when, in the vermilion fleece
Over your forehead, salt will appear,
Bitter salt; and like an old abandoned altar
You will buckle in the shadow
Softly, thinking of caresses without number
With which ruddy and brown lovers once covered you.

Everyone's desire soon fades away.
You will count all your days and hours.
In the words they said to you, their kisses and lures,
Time will substitute the names of the dead for the
    living,
And you will say how one was desirable,
And the others loving, and how exorable
And mild to respire sweet life was then!
So, until dawn comes and separates
The ardent night and the enlaced daylight
Of embraces and sobs; do not be miserly,
And no longer count your kisses.
Love me, hug me, prolong my delight;
Until daylight, open wide your charming eyes;
Repose more closely, lean your smooth forehead
On my moist forehead and tell me you are dying!
Oh, my blood is withdrawing and my heart failing;
I gasp while inhaling the odor of our sins
And, killed by amour, as on a battlefield,
All the roads of amour are strewn tonight!

And in the silence the soft voices call to one another
and respond to one another, spelling out the perilous
counsels of their morbid supplication of amour:

Love today; soon the hour will come
When those who say to you: "always,"
Will no longer think about you.

A morose and sad prophecy of which the ecstatic gaze of the king proclaims and loudly cries the lie, but which appears to worry nevertheless the wandering maid of the highways whom an unexpected caprice has placed on the throne.

She does not see the prince in adoration at her feet, any more than she hears the burning intermediary request of the two pages leaning over the gallery of friezes above her head.

A kind of hallucination possesses her, and, straightening in a sort of ecstasy, her great bright eyes fixed on who knows what nostalgic vision, she leans one hand on the violet silken cushions of the platform and the other clasps to her bosom a bouquet of wild flowers. Two campanulas have fallen on to the steps of the throne: two campanulas as blue as her visionary eyes, filled with the mystic blue of some unknown horizon.

In the background, in the frame of the open window, a warm sunlit landscape, a harvest-time landscape, seems gray with dust, as if seen through the bars of a prison cell.

DISTANT ROSES

THE TAPESTRY OF EROS
(*L'Écho de Paris*, 9 September 1892; reprinted in *Le Journal*, 9 May 1896 as "L'Amour brodeur" [Amour the Embroiderer])

For Auguste Lauzet[1]

UNDER the exterior portico of his palace, Seigneur Eros is seated in a cathedra of violet wood; seven steps of porphyry extend gleaming mirrors at the feet of the god in which the white marble of columns is reflected—a white marble scarcely veined with pink, like the bosom of a virgin—the capitals of which, heightened with green gold, stand out brightly against a sky as profoundly blue as the sea.

---

1 When this story first appeared the painter and engraver Marie-Auguste Lauzet (1863-1898) had just published his first book of *Art Impressioniste*, featuring engravings made from paintings by Manet, Monet, Pissarro, Renoir and others. Lauzet lived in Sèvres with the artist Jeanne Jacquemin, and Lorrain met him when he sought her out after seeing the exhibition of her pastels described in "Princesses of Darkness."

A mysterious landscape of waters and mountains, quivering with lakes and broken peaks, with the luminous pylons of glaciers here and there, is framed between the columns of the portico; the paving stones of the palace are strewn with branches of myrtle and oleander, and, at intervals, frail garlands of periwinkles and ivy link the fluted stems of the columns.

In the cathedra of violet wood encrusted with mat silver and ivory, Seigneur Eros is sitting. He is leaning indolently on heavy cushions of pale silk, with the sumptuous advancement of an awning above his head, and idly tracing chimerical designs with the slender fingers of a long, slow hand on a large tapestry extended on a frame before him.

Balls of wool and hanks of silk are heaped up in a basket at his feet; a thin needle is shining in the canvas and he, while singing fragments of refrains, continues to apply the sharp point of a golden quill delicately to the weave.

And under the tip of that strange stylet, the forms of flowers and animals appear, indicating by means of a red line on the whiteness of the canvas palms, sheaves of crimson lilies, trees, wild beasts and, in places, human individuals, adorable landscapes and scenes of amour. The god, who is taking pleasure in giving substance to his dreams, sometimes takes the needle and, letting go of the stylet, embellishes the design with colored wool; then he takes up the quill again, and puts it down again in order to search between the heavy cushions for a little oval mirror, and smiles therein with his gaze and his lips for a moment.

And, in fact, what image more delightful than his own could he contemplate? Of what appearance could he dream more charming than his supple nudity of an ephebe in that feminine robe, so delicately mauve and striped with dark green, in its silver frame?

Of a childlike and perverse beauty with his large shadowed eyes, simultaneously glaucous and violet, like his robe, and the ambiguous mystery of his mouth, his mouth of a laughing and savant carnivore, he attracts like a danger and troubles like a threat; he has caresses in his eyes and cruelty in his fashion of displaying his teeth, and then, suddenly—for everything about him is as mobile as the sea—it is the smile that intoxicates tenderly while the gaze, having become metallic, chuckles and shines ferociously.

But see the grace and the languor of those attitudes, the breaking of that almost feminine waist, from which one senses the torso rearing up so swiftly, the deliberate lassitude of his bare arms, which trail like scarves and launch death so surely! How pitilessly they draw a bow, those weary fingers of an embroiderer, momentarily occupied with wool and a mirror; oh, the seductiveness and enervating mildness of all that deceptive being, and, on the pink brocade of the awning and the cathedra embroidered with birds and arabesques, the golden flecks of his hair, as short and curly as waves, that yellow fleece in which three strings of pearls fix a tiger's claw between the eyebrows and a flower in the covert of the ear.

He came three times to the spring.
And then, one evening, returned no more.

29

And with a regular, rhythmic movement, Seigneur Eros plunges his needle, fixes its point, and, with a song on his lips, fills the design of the canvas with subtle nuances.

> *When dawn has appeared in full,*
> *The handsome archer with the blond hair*
> *Returns to sit down by the window,*
> *And the breeze shakes loose confessions.*

And in the coming and going of his slim bare arms, the profound blue sky is resplendent between the marble shafts; on the shiny paving stones the oleanders embalm, and in the overwhelming heat of midday, further aggravated by the agony of the flowers, the god busies himself around his tapestry without even glancing at two human forms asleep across the steps of the throne at his feet.

> *They love one another well, however,*
> *And the moon in the depths of the clearings*
> *Sees them wandering all springtime long;*
> *The autumn is harsh for the primroses.*

> *What struck the gaze at first,*
> *Was, lying in the flowers,*
> *His lover, and the golden cup*
> *In which her soul had dissolved.*

And behold, leaning over the basket of balls of wool, he now brings out hues, and in a muted voice, as if speaking in a dream:

Lifting on his trembling arm
The head of the unfortunate,
He placed his burning forehead there
And took the poisoned cup.

He took the cup and drained it,
Then, lying on the embalmed grass,
Very gently, he expired
Next to the beloved corpse.

And now, repressing a yawn, the god lets himself sink backwards, collapsing among the cushions of the cathedra; and, suddenly becoming pale and languid, he pushes the frame away with the tip of his finger, sticks his needle in the canvas, stretches himself and stammers: "I'm sleepy; continue, you others," and, touching with his quill the shoulders of the two pages lying at his feet, he closes his eyes, relaxes and falls asleep.

Seigneur Eros goes to sleep and his two companions awake; oh, what a strange and sinister expression the two pages of Seigneur Eros have! Without a drop of blood beneath the skin, with the disquieting pallor of linen, eyelids burned and bruised, feverish livid hands, impatient clenched hands, have immediately taken possession of the needles and the wool, and are busy, hastening in silence around the frame, the weave of which fills with violent colors and livid shades.

The embroiderer to the right, with the heart-rending face of the crucified, his poor cheeks sticky with tears, with a strange bewildered gaze in his pale eyes, stifles great sighs as he works, which inflate his adolescent bosom fully; he embroiders while keeping obstinately lowered a head that is still adorably young, but permanently scored by the sharp fingernail of suffering.

He is Regret!

The other, with hair of ardent red, so red that it seems bloody, is even grimmer; his staring somber eyes are blazing with a bleak glare, as if withdrawn beneath thick black eyebrows, and in his white face, as pale as a host, dry red lips twist a smile that sniggers and curses; there are threats in his gaze and blasphemies in his mouth, but he is robust and strong, his knotty fingers plunge the needle angrily into the canvas of Eros; it is with punches that he seems to be carrying out his task, his mute and menacing task, and at every point that he makes, the god's tapestry becomes crimson, the somber crimson of coagulated blood, like punctured flesh, and they are wounds that the sinister page is hollowing out with his needle, as if with a dagger.

He is Despair!

He is wedged into a narrow leotard of black cloth decorated with the green leaves of nettles and draped proudly in the rags of an old scarlet mantle, for he is vain and proud of his ever-renewed anguish and the ancient royalty of his eternal dolor.

He is Despair!

And under the agile hands, the tapestry of Eros is covered with lamentable designs and lugubrious scenes; the wools and the silks that were sparkling and fresh a little while ago between the fingers of the god now seem tinted with the juice of hemlock and euphorbia; they have become green-tinted and venomous, and the lividity of the flowers blooming on the canvas is reminiscent of a field of poisons.

And yet, in his cathedra encrusted with mat silver, Seigneur Eros, asleep, is respiring so peacefully and seems to be smiling at such pleasant dreams. Crouched at his feet, his two sinister pages finish the task that he commenced, Despair, with his harsh, staring eyes and Regret, with his soft, weary eyes, both of them absent from the palace, carried far away, very far away toward an obsessive and painful thought; and while, without exchanging a word, without even consulting one another with a glance, the taciturn companions are busy around their master's frame, the sun, which is decreasing and beginning to sink behind the mountains, has suddenly illuminated an unknown corner of the landscape: the unexpected crease of a valley in which, in the middle of a garden of cypresses, all the tombs and crosses loom up of a white cemetery.

LORELEY
(*L'Écho de Paris*, 7 October 1892)

For Henry Bauer[1]

"DEATH to the witch, the whore to the gibbet!" The jeers and the clamors rose up accusingly from the stone balconies encumbered with townspeople and the obscure vaults of the cornmarket, where a host of mounted archers was assembled, amid the whinnying of horses, and fists were extended toward the town hall, where the cortege had just stopped.

---

1 Henry Bauer (1851-1916), an illegitimate son of Alexandre Dumas, was sent to New Caledonia after fighting for the Commune, during which he had formed a lasting friendship with Louise Michel. He returned to Paris in 1879 when granted a belated amnesty; he made his living thereafter as a polemical journalist, becoming an influential critic, a significant supporter of Richard Wagner and Émile Zola; he was on the original staff of the *Écho de Paris* and was a significant promoter of its extravagant use of short fiction; unlike the paper's editor-in-chief, the conservatively-inclined Valentin Simond, he was a fervent defender of all liberal causes, including so-called "decadent" literature, in which context he championed Oscar Wilde and Alfred Jarry as well as Lorrain and the other members of the *Écho* stable.

At the foot of the staircase, where brutal hands had pushed her, Lore had fallen to her knees, stumbling in the pleats stiff pleats of yellow brocade of her dress embroidered with anemones of pink gold and lilies of green gold; her heavy silken tresses had flowed from beneath her head-dress over her cheeks and her shoulders, and, reminiscent of a drowned women under the scattered russet sparks of her fleece, her mouth agape and her eyes fixed, she had instinctively extended her two arms before her and was now clinging to the governor's knees.

But he, having disengaged himself from the young woman's bare arms, had made a sign to the lansquenets to take her down two steps, and, without looking any longer at the creature crouching a few paces away, her back shaking in the flowers of her dress with the frightful tremor of a hunted beast, he had begun to speak in a loud voice:

"Who among you, noble, bourgeois or laborer, was in the abode of this young woman last night? What did he see? Let him come forward boldly and say what he knows: the brawl, the combatants, the how and the why, the hour and the place. I'm listening."

And from the square where the rabble of the town was assembled, vociferating and growling menacingly, a rumor rose up such that the herald standing next to the governor had to raise his trumpet to his mouth and repeat the appeal three times.

Curiosity caused faces to flow to the mullioned windows of the tall stout houses; there was an accumulation of heads on every floor, and all the way to the roofs disappointed gestures indicated from afar the wretched young woman collapsed and mute at Monseigneur's feet, whom murmurs were already accusing.

An old soldier finally emerged from the ranks and advanced awkwardly. He had witnessed the brawl; it was about midnight, they were drunk, their tankards empty, and they were about to leave; a throw of the dice—my God, yes, an accursed throw of the dice—which was to decide the night and who would remain to sleep with the whore, had led to the quarrel, for the slut was one of those that a man could not look at twice without his loins stirring and being inflamed. When one is drunk, the hands are prompt. How it had come to blows was self-explanatory. But as the girl was frightened by the naked blades, they had gone out into the square to talk, without a candle, and, well, there had been a certain amount of stabbing and a massacre under the balcony, in her honor. The girl, half-dead herself, had cried help and murder, but servants had bolted all the doors. In the morning, the threshold of the house was found red, with the cadavers of ten fine young men sprawling, their skin run through.

He did not know anything else, except that until then the girl had always lived without scandal and reclusively, closely surveyed by her gallants, who only let her go out on feast days . . . assuredly reckless in her body and hotter in dalliance than any other but incapable of molesting anyone—entirely to the contrary . . .

And a formidable laughter had shaken the square, the rabble applauding the soldier's story.

Lore, still crouching and stupid, thought she heard the governor mutter then the words *in pace, the pyre* and *honorable amends,* and after an *away from here, witch, it's in Rome that it's necessary to purge your case* he had gone back up the steps of the town hall and, his expression malevolent, had disappeared into the hall, followed by his escort, delivering the young woman to the people.

Then hands had seized her again and forced her to stand up; livid and half-mad, Lore found herself alone in the middle of the crowd, a noisy crowd unfurling around her like the waves of the sea. Lifted up, drawn from the steps in the open air, through streets and squares swarming with a growling population drunk on cries of death, she had closed her eyes and abandoned herself to the arms that were carrying her, unable to catch her breath and only returning to herself semi-consciously, standing under the porch of the old cathedral, its vault saddened by drapes of mourning.

There, dominating a large flock of incense-burners, a man was seated in the depths of an immense nave: a tall mitered old man, with the advancement of the baldaquin of a dais above his head—a bishop—and the nave was black with people . . .

In the shadow sewn with candlelight, five trestles surrounded by women at prayer could be glimpsed behind the railings of the choir, and a kind of protracted sob was audible under the vaults with golden dots, gasped like a death-rattle, backed by chanting voices intoning the office for the dead. And Lore, still pushed by the crowd, having penetrated the railings, and having been tilted over the heads of the women, suddenly stopped, shivering; a great cold seemed to have seized her, and her teeth were chattering beneath her unkempt tresses, for on the five trestles, illuminated by the candles, ten biers were aligned, the biers of ten young men massacred for her during the night's slaughter. Then a great cry of distress made the windows tremble; Lore had just collapsed, her face against the flagstones, at the very foot of the bishop's forbidden dais.

Her shoulders and her breasts had almost emerged from the bodice of her dress, and, her forehead in the dust, she now accused herself, sobbing and demanding that she be put to death, but begging that before anything else she be taken outside the cathedral, far from those candles and those coffins . . . Those canticles were making her ill, that incense was choking her, for she was a witch, she confessed it now, her lovers had loved her too much and she cursed her past and the sin of her life; and her heels beat the mosaic of the choir with precipitate thrusts, and her strangled voice implored them to take her outside.

The bishop had quit his throne, and, believing her to be possessed, tried to impose his hands in that beautiful female body contorted by despair; the deacons climbed on to the seats of the stall in order to see, and the heads of curiosity-seekers were crushed against the railings around the choir. The bishop having asked the visionary whether she had parents, a voice in the crowd rose up, which responded: "Seigneur, she has no mother and lives alone; that's Lore." The bishop shivered, for the pale *fille de joie* had not struck his eyes before.

Then the man of God, seized by a great sadness, said: "Let another condemn you if he dares; I will not have you put to death. Go into a cloister, shave that culpable hair; bury forever in shadow the snow of those arms and that proud face, which commands amour; extinguish the gleam of those blue eyes, in which a charm of desire reigns that is perilous to the salvation of men, for I sense in spite of myself the sweetness of a caress and an attraction that is a trap of Hell. That is the only punishment I impose upon you: night and silence upon your beauty of a famous courtesan, and forgetfulness of the scandal."

And, having turned away from the creature collapsed before him, in the moist clarity of her tresses, loosened like a pool of gold, he plunged, solemn and pensive, into the shadow and the glimmer of the master altar ablaze with candles.

Now, her forehead humiliated, she was descending a dusty and shadowless street alongside the ramparts of the town; behind her, three huge ruddy men-at-arms trailed, their backs rounded beneath their halberds, forming an escort: a mute and tragic group.

Sometimes, along the ruined walls, a breach opened up, florid with violets, through which wheat and other crops could be seen, and the Rhine snaking through the countryside, and the men called a halt in order to draw breath, at ease by virtue of a gust of breeze in the calcined street—for it was August and the sun was very hot. She continued walking, silent and bleak, a coarse mantle thrown over the luminous brocade of her dress and her heavy hanging tresses.

Neither pardon nor justice mattered to her now; had not everyone—the governor and the bishop himself, in his apparent pity, even the cloister open to the belated repentance of scoundrels and the worst highway robbers—rejected her and driven her away, too beautiful to live and yet too beautiful to die?

Spared by a priest and denied by a people, that was what a world implacable toward the innocents it doomed had decreed for her. Do you know where she was going now, bare-headed under the leaden sun, as if annihilated in the green gold and pink gold flowers of her trailing robe, that woman whose eyes were staring straight ahead? To a leprosarium, and this was what the future of Loreley would be henceforth: to grow old in the midst of lepers, in abandonment and insanitary filth, to bandage purulent wounds and clean ulcers.

Around her the hedges are full of chirping nests, and poppies are blooming in the wheat—for the city is already far behind them, its enclosing wall having disappeared; a stronger breeze is making the rye and the oats rustle, and the three men-at-arms, whose silhouettes are profiled and magnified in black against a coppery sky, can already see the city's roofs and pointed bell-towers descending behind the horizon like the castles and keeps that one sees depicted on a gold background in missals and stained-glass windows.

Then she pauses; at a bend in the road the Rhine has just appeared—the Rhine of her childhood, like a strip of quicksilver between the quivering reeds of its banks. Suddenly, tottering like a drunken woman, Lore has stopped, seized again by scattered memories of years of old, the soothing charm of forgotten things; and from the city, already distant, and its slate belfries and its disheveled ramparts, her entire past surges forth, smiling and resplendent; firstly there is the paternal dwelling, an old house full of shadow and silence, lost in the depths of an outlying district; the grandfather, a tall bald old man forever huddled in a corner of the hearth, with his chilly gestures; then the bedroom with hexagonal windows decorated with crimson fleurs-de-lys, as many joyful flames, which the awakening of every new dawn filled with exuberance; the pot of basil in the corner of the little window; then the first lover, afterwards the young lansquenet with the unruly moustache, a captain, and then an alderman, and then another, and others still. Where were the lilies of her virginal couch lying now, their petals shed and withered? She was everyone's whore, accursed and scorned by all.

Then, having turned to the three men-at-arms, who had stopped behind her, Lore still had the strength to implore those rough soldiers, and having detached the heavy golden chains from her bare shoulders and the bracelets studded with enamels from her arms, she said to them, in a voice so soft that one might have thought that one was hearing a soul mourn and weep: "Will you allow me to contemplate one last time the walls of my city; these few jewels and golden chains will compensate you for the delay; it is a last adieu, the supreme wish of an exile. Before the sun sets behind those mountains I would like to climb on to that rock overlooking the river for a moment, and gaze from there one last time, in order to carry away in my eyes the country from which I am departing; it is a foolish caprice that will make you smile, but of which my soul is dying. Tell me, will you do that?"

And while she spoke, her eyes, the ardent eyes of a torture victim, had become soft again, attractive and dominating, as in the time when, a concubine adored by margraves and dukes, she poured out the intoxication of her beauty, like a philter, to the lust of a people; and the three men-at-arms responded affirmatively.

Having then climbed on to the rock, Lore smiled at her executioners, and, standing as if in a nimbus in the molten gold of the sunset and the fluid gold of her hair, spreading over the golden thread of her dress, she said: "Since there is neither justice nor pardon for me, I am quitting you and I absolve you, infamous world that has doomed me, and which reproaches me today for my beauty as for a crime; I absolve you and I am coming to you, consolatory death!"

And having folded her arms over her breast, the beauty leaned forward in a dream above the river and let herself fall, her face ecstatic.

The three ruddy men-at-arms, crouching in the shadow of the rock, weighed Loreley's jewels in their hands.

A PRIMITIVE

(*L'Écho de Paris*, 25 October 1892; reprinted in
Le Journal 11 June 1896 as "Les Errants" [The
Wanderers])

For Madame Jeanne Jacquemin

IN a landscape of sands and dead waters, where one
senses that the soil is forever sterile and the wind
bitter, a lamentable and sumptuous group is advancing.
Interminable routes have brought into the heart of these
marshes that knight helmed like Saint George and the
two wretched women whose flight he seems to be pro-
tecting and whose weakening march he is sustaining,
mercifully leaning over his saddle-bow with an arm
passed around the waist of one of them as she stumbles.

A kind of wind of exile ripples the surface of the pale
stagnant waters, and an angry sky weighs upon the distant horizon of dunes, dismal and stifling. The redness
of bloody wounds appears at intervals between the ashy
clouds, and the sea, glimpsed beyond the ultimate undulations of the sand, resembles a band of green gold in that
strange twilight.

The dolorous and tragic group drags itself through the sad landscape of taciturn waters and silence; the two women are barefoot and their wan faces with profound rings around their magnified eyes testify to a frightful lassitude. Oh, those poor naked feet, harassed and bruised, the flesh of which is burned and the skin bleeding! How many shores have they trodden, for how many years have they skirted unquiet seas in the grim hostility of evenings? How many dead leaves have they stirred and how many stones, stopping by turns in the bosom of the brambles and the freshness of the mosses of the countries traveled? On how many doors have those feverish and tremulous hands knocked, and how many times have they been held out in vain before finally dangling along their bodies, so desperately inert and heart-rending, those pale lips fixed in a kind of sublime immobility? From what wellspring of bitterness must they have drunk in order to learn that terrible smile of resignation?

Oh, those suppliant faces, of martyrs mute in agony, the painful and weary attitudes of the poor bodies that can do no more, of beggars or banished princesses!

Beggars? No, for the sumptuous robes, heavy with embroideries, fall like capes over their poor bare feet, and silken mantles with cameo clasps weigh upon their shoulders, and their long, unkempt hair runs in golden streams dotted with precious stones, burdened with diadems in the form of tiaras studded with gems and bright enamels.

They resemble two sisters, but one is still resisting while the other is succumbing. Without the compassionate helmeted knight who is leaning over, sustaining her with one arm, and without her vigilant companion,

44

who has taken her under the armpits and is guiding her, she would have collapsed on the road a long time ago; and yet she is animated by kind of somber ardor, a sort of tragic ecstasy, which transfigures that bloodless face of a torture victim and puts a mysterious flame into the wandering of her dark eyes.

She is Suffering!

The blood of seven wounds has stained the golden brocade of her robe bright crimson, and if the weave is so stiff it is because, for more than a thousand years, the wretch has been roaming randomly, exiled and expelled from everywhere; the warm blood would have dried up if the wound itself had not ceased to leak, gradually enlarged, for more than a thousand years, bleeding and weeping in the hearts of the poor, of mothers and lovers, crying and suffering for more than a thousand years in the flesh of the weak and the oppressed.

The powerful and the fortunate of this world do not want to know her; for a long time she had worn away her knees on the thresholds of their palaces; the church sometimes deigned then to serve as a refuge, but mitered prelates, and the Popes with them, ended up forbidding her the porches of cathedrals to which she had long been admitted to pray, huddled in a corner with the lepers and beggars on crutches, at the bottom of the steps.

The crimson of her cape obfuscated the eyes of adulterous queens and sacrilegious emperors; her silent shadow obscured the brightness of feast days and royal baptisms; and since then she has been going about the world, crushed by the hatred of everyone, without a roof to shelter her head, rejected from the hovels of manual laborers as from the castles of lords, showered with insults, soiled by ignominy, proscribed by cities and jeered in the country, a fallen queen, desperate and mute, only accompanied by Pity: Pity, who sustains her and comforts her in silence, with the tenderness of her smile and the support of her beautiful hands. her beautiful merciful hands, as delicate and tender as a silken mantle; Pity, whose bare feet bleed like hers but who only sees and feels the wounds of Suffering; healing Pity, the Pity that sympathizes in the twilight, without anyone seeing her, the aged pauperesses belated on the roadside, and who astonishes them with the affectionate smile of her eyes; Pity, who knows how heavy the beech-wood faggot is on shoulders clad in coarse cloth in the evening, and how tenacious the mud is in clinging to poor weary feet; Pity, finally, whose damp necklace of sardonyxes and pearls has the touching gleam of tears, and whose gray silk dress, embroidered with anemones, tinkles and quivers so softly under the raindrops in the melancholy of the evening.

Pity is devoted to Suffering, sharing her exile, accepting insults and harsh refusals because of her, with her and for her, and, for love of Suffering, disdaining the tables of palaces to which poets sometimes summon her, where they have often invited her to sit down amid the long-necked amphorae and silver chocolate boxes. And through the sad landscape of dead waters and sands, the two proscribed queens parade with a slow step the sumptuous trains of their embroidered robes and the mysterious aureole of their tiaras and their dolor.

As for the knight helmeted and gauntleted in mat silver who protects them and escorts them, whose shadow is magnified on the sand at their feet, he is so handsome that one might think him a woman; silent, svelte and sorrowful, he is reminiscent of a great sculpted lily, and his bulging silver breastplate has the dull gleam of a dead moon; his black horse is caparisoned with crimson cloth, which the sun and the rain have turned violet, making it resemble a moving amethyst.

Oh, that pale and mute knight with a feminine visage, but an expression so grave in the ashen and sulfurous dusk, in the midst of those sands, only limited by an ocean of green gold! A bouquet is wilting on the iron of his lance, and faded ribbons float from the hilt of his sword, and the footfalls of his horse make no sound, as if stifled by the dust; but the two women and he have the same gaze, the same drowned gaze, varying from the intense blue of his irises to the moist blackness of Suffering's pupils.

He is the knight Melancholy, the champion of the two proscribed queens, the companion of the exile of the two plaintive ladies, whom he no longer wants to quit.

Out there in the distance, at the limit of the landscape, on the edge of the metallic and gilded sea, a castle raises its crenellated mass, flanked with keeps and towers: a brand new castle in the middle of the sands, a feudal domain whose turrets of brick and roofs of slate are resplendent in an oblique sunbeam falling between the clouds. The postern is wide open and a joyous oriflamme of bright silk is undulating at the summit of one of its corner-turrets, inviting the three vagabonds to enter.

There is a good welcome and good shelter therein; they, who are expelled and rejected everywhere, will find something to drink and somewhere to sleep, and all three know it—and yet, all three continue their dolorous route, all three turning their backs to the rich and splendid domain. None of the three—the bleeding Suffering no more than the tender Pity or their sad and gentle knight, Melancholy—wants to halt there momentarily, although God knows how great their thirst is, how ardent their fever, how weary their flesh and how troubled their souls.

But the castle is that of Forgetfulness, and none of them wants to forget.

TIPHAINE
(*L'Écho de Paris*, 24 February 1893)

For Henri de Régnier[1]

Tiphaine, at midnight on the edge of ditches
Was wandering by moonlight, and the pink heather,
Raising its flowers on its stems, kissed her hands.

THE valets in service had taken away the dishes, the venisons as well as the honeyed buckwheat cakes, the pages had brought the greyhounds from the kennels, and in the high-ceilinged hall, barely illuminated by the torches suspended in the rings in the wall, it was the time when the old seigneur, with his elbows on the arms of his waxed wooden stall, plunged into bleak remembrance of the past.

---

1 Henri de Régnier (1864-1936), who became one of the leading Symbolists of the *fin-de-siècle*, was still in the first phase of his career when this story was written and had not yet published the collections of prose—translations of which are included in the sampler *A Surfeit of Mirrors* (2012)—that helped to establish his reputation.

Outside, in accordance with the season, there was all the enchantment of moonlight over the fields of green wheat and heather of May, of the bellowing of squalls running over the crests of the waves, and sometimes flocks of blinded seagulls arriving with packets of rain and gusts of spray collided with the window panes; on those nights all of the wooden beams in the old town besieged by November creaked lamentably, and the ironwork of the heavy doors resounded, and through the interminable corridors of the fortress there was something like the noise of anvils, and sinister groans: an entire sabbat of souls in distress, which made the watchman huddled in his lodge sweat with fear and kept the men-at-arms in service in the hall of the manor awake, with lugubrious thoughts within their skulls.

But whether the squalls were raging, sweeping the snow of December and the dead leaves of October into the ditches of the old domain, or the moonlight of June was playing gently over the round-path and discovering in eccentric moving silhouettes the wallflowers of the battlements, it was for old Bertrand Du Guesclin,[1] in

---

1 Bertrand Du Guesclin (c1320-1380) was a famous Breton knight and oft-victorious military commander, who fought on the side of the French (and thus against Breton nationalists) in the Hundred Years War. For the last ten years of his life he was Charles V's Constable de France. In 1363 or thereabouts he married Tiphaine Raguenel, their union often being cited as an exemplar of courtly love in troubadour ballads, in which she is represented as beautiful and knowledgeable in occult arts, whereas her notoriously ugly husband was illiterate. A depiction of the wedding of Bertrand and Tiphaine by the writer and illustrator Paul de Semant (1855-1915) is still available as a print, and might have been the inspiration for the present story. When he wrote the story, Lorrain could not

winter as in summer, in spring as in autumn, the worst
hour of all, the hour haunted by regrets and dreams of
the past, the hour of specters, with that hostess of old
men, Sorrow, behind them, and in her shadow, fear of
the future; and there was also, in the meditation of the
old melancholy hall, the memory of long vigils far into
the night and the silence, and the isolation of Comte
Bertrand with his memories: the memories that sometimes surged forth with the faces of long ago, with muted
sandals, in the embrasure of some low door. And the somnolent old sire then had the vision of vague individuals
with heavy eyes and sealed lips leaning on their elbows
on the arms of the stalls of the perimeter, and the names
of former companions in arms, once clamored in the fire
of battles or stammered in the tender drunkenness of
feasts, buzzed in his ears; and in the weave of the long
tapestries figures of dream appeared, whose gestures and
smiles he recognized, distant hours rising again from the
past, with the flowers of youth in their hands, but their
gold and silk tarnished now . . . and the old man awoke
then, his long face hollowed out by deeper wrinkles, and
putting his poor old hands together, he let a large tear
run down his wan cheek, and sighed: "Tiphaine."

Tiphaine! And above the visions of iron and blood
of his warrior years, red battlefields strewn with cadavers under angry skies, fiery and bleak, the sack of towns
resounding with the jeers of the victors and the screams

---

know that a ruined house on Mont Saint-Michel would be falsely
attributed to Tiphaine in the early twentieth century, and that a
skull fancifully imagined to be hers would be excavated there in the
early twenty-first.

of slaughtered populations, triumphant entries under the undulating pleats of banners, with steel shields at the elbow and lances in hand, to the sound of festival bells and flag-laden streets, forced marches in the moonlight and nocturnal ambushes in the rain in the quivering rushes of ponds . . . above all that, the mild and floating face of a young woman was evoked: a svelte lady of pensive grace with beautiful hands bearing alms; and the blonde Tiphaine, whose smiles and caresses had embalmed and rejuvenated his fortieth year, gradually reappeared before him.

As if captive between the blue trees of the tapestry, she smiled between the gnarled branches bearing the yellow apples of fabulous forests dreamed by the embroiderers; marvelous birds with dazzling plumage fluttered around her head, and it really was her bright eyes, translucent and blue, that were staring at him, as it really was her bare feet that were shining softly on the grass, in the tangle of enormous and sumptuous flowers.

Tiphaine! And in his heart of an old chief of partisans, he saw her again such as she had appeared to him the first time, sitting by a spring on the edge of an ancient forest.

It was one evening, a little before nightfall, and the shadow of the wood was invading the heath, where brief gleams were zigzagging in places, final reflections of daylight on the gilt of furze, dying away in the darkness. The air was so mild and so strangely poignant that Du Guesclin, then in his prime, almost had to do himself violence in order not to faint; it was then that he had perceived her. Sheathed in a long ash-gray dress, with a mantle of pink linen embroidered with anemones clasped over her shoulders, she was sitting still, her elbow on the rim of a small fountain in the form of a well; white forms were pressing around her with a silky sound, and in a flutter of wings the comte had recognized a flock of wild geese extending the simultaneous effort of their necks toward the unknown woman.

Although seated, she had appeared to him to be very tall, even gigantic, and, rude soldier as he was, he had stopped, hesitantly, before that strange crepuscular silhouette profiled, as if luminous, against that savage heath, magnified by the darkness.

He hesitated again when the unknown woman, having got up from the stone bench on which she was sitting, had greeted him by his name, in a voice so soft that he had imagined that he was hearing the water of the well speaking. "In future, handsome sire de Tombelaine," she had said, "I shall wait for you here every evening of my life, as I am this evening." And, all the geese having risen from the ground with little cries, the lady had appeared momentarily to be enveloped by a white turbulence of wings, with a sudden splendor of precious stones and gems in the yellow silk of her hair and the embroideries of her mantle fastened with rubies.

And every evening he had returned there, as if brought back by the hand to the edge of that flowery heath, where, simply by virtue of seeing the sun set again behind the lady's shoulders and her mantle of rose linen softly illuminated by the ultimate reflection, he felt as if a fruit were dissolving in his heart; and there were three months of tender rendezvous and delightful waiting, until the night of Saint John when, in the twilight of the great rejuvenated wood, it was given to him to go in quest, to the sound of lutes and flutes, of the beautiful bride, ornamented and adorned like the reliquary of Saint Anne, to stand on the ruined threshold of the paternal manor.

Oh, that return through the thickets of the ancient forest, bathed in moonlight, the troubling incense of hawthorn and the unconscious caress of the mosses on which their feet lingered, and the profound gaze of periwinkles, as if awakened with a start, between the snaky coils of roots at the foot of the green oaks of the slopes; all the enchantment of those haunted woods, that night of songs, music, silken banners and errant torches; and, through the ravines and the clearings, conducting the white-clad bride in her linen veil to the seigneurial domain of the husband.

And now, through the wools and the frayed gold of the long tapestries, he saw again the nuptial procession passing, the deacons in stoles and the priests in chasubles, beneath the fringes of the awning, the sheets of light in the braided hair of the young women, friends of the betrothed couple, the long stems of lilies in their hands surrounded by green box, and the handsome squires leading dogs on leashes, and the soldiers with rude faces beneath morions, garlanded as a sign of celebration, and the laughing pink-cheeked children holding sheaves of fennel, lavender and irises against their bellies, some of them, emboldened, astride the backs of a few mastiffs, and the trailing dresses of the ladies, and the hennins of the demoiselles and the caps of the musicians, and the bearers of candles setting the blue-tinted darkness of the forest ablaze with light, and the cavaliers clad in fur, and the flashes of moonlight on their stirrups.

Tiphaine! He saw her again as a chatelaine in the dwelling, a saint in the chapel and a housekeeper in the gynaeceum, in the midst of her women, spinning wool and embroidering fine gold thread, and whether she was idling in the middle of the interior courtyard of the castle, paved with black marble, or she appeared at the corner of some country path in the tall shadow of ripe wheat, coming through the crops to meet him, accompanied by some juvenile page carrying a satchel or gifts of nature for the needy, it was always the great hennin of a noble and powerful lady that he saw surmounting that pensive and charming visage with lowered eyelids and a rosy ingenuous smile: her hennin, the color of saffron and honey, almost the hue of her tresses, the strange coiffure of a magicienne, with the double fall of veils that the slightest breeze agitated like two wings, and which always seemed to envelop her with he knew not what invisible flight.

And over her footsteps the brocatelle of her armoried robe snaked and rustled, sometimes disquieting.

Oh, that undulating train with the flexibility of a snake, as if it were belying the motionless prayer of the hennin, pointing like a bell-tower toward the sky! But he had lent an ear to the suspicious words of his old chaplain, and the pusillanimous monk had poured into his heart the poison of mistrust, the mistrust that withers amour and dries up good faith.

Bizarre, in fact, had been the encounter with that unknown woman in the troubled hour of dusk, in that solitary place, ill-famed because of the well once consecrated to the evil gods, nymphs and spirits that the Gospel had dispersed, and that sudden amour, like a malign fever, and the languors that had followed, the force that had brought him back every evening, involuntarily, even his name, pronounced by the lady in a seductive voice of speaking water, and that flock of geese, phantoms so rapidly evaporated in the darkness—all of that contained magic and charms, and he had struggled, captive of some maleficent amour, caught in net of a demon or a fay.

And, intoxicated with fear by the monk, he had been able to follow his fearful counsel and suspect the gentle and devoted lady. "By night she deserts your bed; she goes into the open country by means of ancient posterns that are thought to be sealed and, accompanied by a dwarf with a monstrous head, who parts the nettles and the wild herbs in her steps she collects hemlock on the tombs of lepers and makes the mandrakes sing."

And, mad with horror and curiosity, he had wanted to see her and to follow her one evening, but he had not had to spy on her for long, for scarcely had they arrived on the edge of the village, on the very threshold of the arched door that opened on to the fields, when the beautiful lady had said, turning toward him: "Never again then, handsome sire de Tombelaine, will I wait for you every evening as on the eve of today, for the knell of death has sounded for Tiphaine; you have suspected me—adieu."

And while he agonized in anguish and terror, his hands flat against the wall of the little stairway, she had vanished into the white country of the moon; something like a sound of wings had quivered, and he had never seen her again.

Tiphaine!

THE IDIOTS OF MALHANTÔT
(*L'Écho de Paris*, 19 & 21 April 1893)

For Madame Shurman[1]

A branch of an apple tree in flower—a delicate at-tention and a precious gift of an American friend to me, a son of Normandy already emigrated to Paris for several years—each flower of which, dotting the gray bark like a rose-tinted snowflake, provides a hint of brightness within the frame of the old tapestries of my work-room, amid the odors of camphor and vetiver of the curtains, finally unfolded after three months of absence: a fresh and delicate odor, of meadows and or-chards. And now, by virtue of respiring and aspiring it, I am invaded by memories of my homeland, the familiar landscapes of the Normandy to which I no longer go,

---

1 It is not obvious who this lady might have been, although there was a poet active at the time who signed herself Anna Shurman. On the other hand, it might be worth noting that a skit by the younger Poquelin was published in *Gil Blas* on 3 September 1896 in which an impresario named Shurman attempts unsuccessfully to lure Liane de Pougy out of an advertised retirement.

freshly evoked and steeped in the perpetual humidity of the sea—and with them, a legend returns to my memory, a poor petty legend of my childhood, a naïve tale redolent of bent knees and joined hands, such as scholars and archeologists were still discovering twenty years ago in the portals of village churches or the faded stained-glass of the rose-windows of the choir.

Her name was Audeberthe and his was Aldric. They had grown up together on the slope of a hill covered with gorse and furze, the moving gold of which was tinted white in April by the snowy flowers of wild apple trees; for the people of their poor hamlet were so primitive and empty-headed, always leaning, as they had been for centuries, over their fishing-nets or their plowshares, that they had never even thought of ameliorating the gnarled trunks of their orchards with grafts, and the cider they drank, as bitter and foamy as the surf of the sea, raked the throat and stung the tongue.

For twenty leagues around the people of other villages turned away in derision from those of Audeberthe and Aldric's hamlet—the idiots of Malhantôt as they were called in the region: Malhantôt, where the girls were so stupid that on moonlit nights in the month of June they went in a troop to bathe in the fields of flax in flowers; Malhantôt, where the Christians had brains so obtuse and so obdurate to the comprehension of texts that the bells of their church, weary of summoning the deaf, had abandoned them, and the curé had followed their example, despairing of preaching to their souls.

That was said of Malhantôt and its peasants throughout the country, and the fact is that the poor folk were the most ragged on the entire coast; for them the sea had fewer fish and the earth fewer grains; their fields were sickening to behold in October, swarming with pebbles, and their crops were pitiful in August, so many mallows and poppies sprouted there instead of wheat and rye; as for the fields of flowering flax, it was mostly thyme and thistles that grew on their land, and while the first saying was as deceptive as a provost's oath, there was truth in the second; the bells had not exactly abandoned Malhantôt and its population of simpletons, but out of stupidity and fear, ever since the appearance of Norse pirates on the coast, the Malhantôtais had submerged them, burying them in the glaucous mystery of the waters along with the sacred ornaments, the ciboria, chalices and petty treasure of the church, in order to hide them from the rapacity of the pirates, and their belfry had remained mute and bleak above an altar devoid of priests and a choir where no masses were sung. The bell-tower of Malhantôt fell into ruin; even the swallows, which are birds beloved by God and which delight in holy ringing, had deserted it; bats nested there and in the evening, at dusk, between the golden brown of wallflowers, there were heavy zigzagging flights of hairy and diabolical wings, for which the believers were regretful.

Poor believers of Malhantôt, it was necessary for them, in order to hear mass on Sundays and feast days, to trudge for leagues through woods and crops, in hot sunlight in summer and snow in winter, to reach some distant church in a hostile village, and attend the office outside, kneeling under the porch, in the midst of gibes about mad girls and nasty boys, for everywhere people made a game of not letting them into the nave, those idiots of a land without bells. Even the most devoted of them, by virtue of being rejected by every Pierre and Jacques, and only catching snatches of the mass and fragments of the sermon, had ended up forgetting the road to the inhospitable sanctuaries, and as the verses of the psalms and the good word were forgotten in Malhantôt, people there fell into disorder, spiritual dissent and fornication.

It was a great affliction to Audeberthe, who had been brought up by a pious grandmother, to see her local church devoid of worship, its bell-tower devoid of bells, and the people with whom she lived akin to pariahs, to accursed dogs scorned by everyone, having become, for the most part, miscreants worthy of malediction.

She was a simple soul, but full of mystery; she had lost her mother when very young and, raised by a plaintive and aged grandmother devoid of teeth, muttering incessantly, babbling prayers, she had grown up in solitude, tête-à-tête with the idea of God. The humble farmhouse where she was born was some way from the village on the edge of the ancient forest of Rouvray, which came to die away after having extended for leagues on the boundary of the region, and Audeberthe had spent the sad years of her early youth guarding her father's geese, standing on a large isolated plateau overlooking a coast of long blue undulations under an eternally gray sky, with the Ocean on one side, and the fleecy waves of the forest of Rouvray on the other, green in spring, yellow in autumn and gray in winter.

Around her, her geese extended their long necks of sacred beasts, and the girl, with a hazel wand in her hand, in the attentive and thoughtful pose of a sculpted figure, listened to the wind moan and whisper, her ear sometimes tilted in the direction of the cliffs and sometimes toward the noisy foliage of the forest, seeking to distinguish the distant sound of bells—of the bells swallowed and submerged for three centuries beneath the waves of the sea or the dormant waters of the pond of Rouvray—for tradition had become obscure on that point, and no one knew exactly where the idiots of Malhantôt had drowned their bells, in the sea or in the pond, and for three hundred years the uncertainty of knowing where to look for the beautiful bronze ladies had thwarted all searches. For three hundred years, only the moon's rays, the rain and the snow had inhabited their abandoned cage.

Legend had conserved the names of the bells—the Bright, the Thunderous and the Argentine—and it was those three names that Aubeberthe's lips stammered and implored perpetually, during her long hours on guard in the midst of the furze on the arid slopes, her ardent eyes of a mystical peasant fixed on the eternal flight of the clouds.

By dint of dreaming about those vanished ladies of bronze, by day on the plateau and by night in her hut, Audeberthe had got it into her head to rediscover them; a conviction had ended up installing itself in her heart that she was the elect of Jesus and Madame Marie, who would discover the hiding place where the three chatterboxes were asleep, and that it was she, Audeberthe, the daughter of Nicolas Sourdois and Mengeotte Lehideux, who would bring the three carilloning ladies back to the bell-tower, restored in celebration, and with them the honesty, wellbeing and the practice of virtues forgotten in the hamlet of accursed dogs.

And in her unbreakable faith, she wandered for long days with an eternal prayer on her lips, her two joined hands placed over her heart, listening to the redemptive sound of the bells vibrate and ring in her inner depths, sometimes indignant at hearing their carillon so clearly in her dream without being able to divine where their sonorous clappers were asleep in the sand, in the reeds or in the seaweed. Were they in the pond of Rouvray or the sea?

When the west wind was raging and the angry Ocean was beating the base of the cliffs with the noise of anvils, Audeberthe thought she could hear the vanished bells panting in the waves; it was their vibration, shaken by the tempest, that was singing mass in the depths of the gulf and resounding in echoes on the beaches—and, faint with joy, Audeberthe knelt down in the midst of her geese, which huddled around her fearfully, and flecks of foam flew over the country, and her unbound hair streaming with salt water sowed white flowers here and there. At other times, especially at the end of March, the east wind ran in abrupt gusts through the valleys and the neighboring forest pricked by the green of the first buds, with a noise like tearing silk. From her solitary plateau, Audeberthe perceived, undulating as far as the eye could see, the violet souls of young shoots, and, like appeals rising from that tender verdure, her ecstatic ear perceived a vague angelus, the sweet chimes of spring festival; and a delectable tenderness inundated her entirely on hearing the Bright and the Argentine ringing gaily alongside the Thunderous, still slumbering at the bottom of the pond, under the warm waters of the April awakening.

But the wind dropped; the voices fell silent in the calm air; vile voices of quarrels between boys and the scandals of girls gone astray rose up from the village all the way to Audeberthe's hut; the bell-tower of the church still remained empty, and a great pity floated within her because of the evil life of the people of her village and the impiety of that godless country, and a great distress also took hold of her. For so long she had had faith and hope in the Lord Jesus and Madame Marie, but springs had succeeded winters and autumns summers without bringing any change to that sad state of souls; and large tears then ran down her brown cheeks, from her eyes of expectation and prayer, which the sea and the sky, contemplated for so long had rendered blue: the profound, changing blue, by turns bright and somber, of blue waves and blue horizons.

The impiety of that village, devoid of bells and devoid of God, which was the great chagrin of Audeberthe, was also the great pain of the heart of Aldric Levillain. In the fifteen years that he had grown up nearby, in the same corner of the forgotten land, he had ended up loving, with a profound and instinctive love, the frail figure of the little girl, standing immutably over his horizons; she had been the first vision of his childhood when, a sickly orphan raised by charity in his uncle's house, his employment had been to scare away the birds fluttering above the sown fields; he spent his days chasing them away by throwing stones at them, his ankles sinking into the mud of the furrows.

One day, one of the stones thrown by the little boy had hit the girl on the temple—a mistake on the part of the guardian of the crops of which Audeberthe bore the scar beneath her hemp-colored tresses. That involuntary harm done to the little goose-girl had filled him with a strange amity for her, a kind of tender veneration that had only increased with the years as they grew older, she increasingly pale and thin in her skirts of strange cloth, he more agile and muscular in his gray cotton cloaks.

In the fifteen years that he had seen her wandering in the sadness of early mornings and the splendor of dusks, or dreaming, her distaff on her bosom and her spindle in her hand, with her back against the spectral silhouette of some old tree trunk, she had ended up entering into his eyes, and from there into his being, so profoundly that he could not detach her from the familiar décor of cliffs and farms. For him she became part of the landscape; she was its errant soul, and its life was incarnated in that slightly awkward and naïve little girl without hips; now that he was grown up and guided a plow, he spent his days behind his uncle's great oxen, pushing into the resistant earth the effort of a heavy plowshare, and an anguish oppressed him when his eyes did not encounter the attentive silhouette of the young spinner at the edge of the fields. The girl was now leading sheep instead of geese, having grown up herself, and her relatives often sent her to graze her flock on the edge of the forest, where the grass grew more densely. On those days, Aldric weighed less heavily on the iron of his plow, and the furrows were hollowed out less deeply, the laborer's thoughts running after the absent shepherdess.

And that was Aldric's great trouble: the gaze of Audeberthe's blue eyes was forever elsewhere, in prayer to Madame Marie or concerned for the bells, the distant eyes always departed into the clouds, when they were not fixed impatiently upon the forest or the sea. His own requested amour in vain, all the ardor of his being rising into his brilliant pupils; Audeberthe did not see them; nor did she hear him, her soul always on the alert for her mysterious bells. Smiling and passive, she abandoned her little rough hands to those of the boy, but her inert fingers did not respond to any grip, and on May evenings, along the hawthorn hedges in flower, when the young laborer, emboldened by spring and solitude, was about to hazard some confession, his voice suddenly choked in his throat and he could no longer find a word to say to that motionless girl with the visionary gaze, who listened to him as if in the depths of a dream; he did not know what eternal prayer was on her lips.

There were minutes when he would have preferred to know that she was dead, days when he would have liked to see those great mysterious eyes, as fresh as cornflowers in the wheat—lying flowers, since they did not want to reveal their secret—close forever. They were soft, those eyes, like the April sky, and as disquieting as the waves; and in the poor little emaciated face of the seeress, burned by the sun, they gleamed strangely, as transparent as water and as pure as the stars.

There were days when he would have liked to be able to dare to put out those eyes.

In the village people mocked the boy, always hankering after the skirts of that simpleton—the Sourdois idiot, as the idiots of Malhantôt called her, by the name of her father. In the evenings, in the flowery pathways, the girls laughed in his face, and on Sundays he dared not go past the inns, ashamed of the nasty remarks of the boys; he was the laughing-stock of the village because of his visible amour for the little shepherdess, whom he ought to have knocked down behind a hedge a long time ago, as the lovers of the region were all accustomed to do with their promises. And a kind of plot was hatched among that coarse and dissolute population against the virginity of Audeberthe, whom all the girls reckless with their bodies would have liked to see pregnant, like them. The sanctity of her pious soul put all those wolves and bitches at bay, and around the naïve idyll there was an unleashing of such base covetousness that the boys took Aldric aside to warn him that they would take charge of the task themselves if he did not do it. After that ignoble threat, the plowboy had indeed surprised more than one equivocal prowler around Audeberthe and her flock, and in the evening, when the shepherdess was taking her sheep back to the animal shed, forms followed her, ducking down beneath the hedges, which the seeress did not see, but whose shadows stabbed poor Aldric with anger and anguish.

Then commenced for the poor fellow such a hard ordeal of jealousy, panic and terror, that after six months of surveillance, maddened by the danger, exasperated by perpetual suspicion and perhaps finally burned by the lust of that land of whores and brewers of children, the plowboy finally decided on the villainous action; and perhaps it was not so much—who knows, O holy lady Marie?—to content his desire or to recover the calm of his heart than to save the frail and gentle Audeberthe from some frightful violence, to avoid the virgin suffering the infamy of a rape or some more atrocious treason.

The Devil, who had obfuscated for sixteen years the innocence of their amour and who wished ardently for their doom, breathed all his malice into the boy's ear; as he feared, for the accomplishment of his evil plan, the mysterious power of Audeberthe's blue eyes, he persuaded Aldric to take the girl into the heart of the forest, to the densest of its thickets of oaks, where the leaves make a green darkness; there, the gaze of the seeress would lose all power, since she would not be able to see, and in order to make the girl follow the boy into the wood, he had the infernal idea of abusing the visionary's state of mind by flattering her mania of recovering the bells.

And so it was that on a bright April morning, the very morning of the holy day of Easter—for the Devil has all audacities, and pleases himself by making God's creatures fall in the hour of the Church's triumph—Aldric approached the pious Audeberthe near the well to which she went every day to draw water for the household, and, leaning on the rim of the well said: "I had a beautiful dream last night, Audeberthe, and may it please God that it was true, for my torments would be over." And as the girl raised her large eyes the color of water to look at him, he went on: "I have seen them, your bells, the Bright, the Thunderous and the Argentine, for which you look out every day, and by night too; I have seen them traversing the calm air, all three of them, in order of size; they were coming back from Rome with the other bells, those of Norties-les-Audraies, those of Manneville, Naucotte and Viport; There were all the bells there of churches for twenty leagues around; they were coming back from Rome and returning to their bell-towers, a true procession in the air, and do you know where our three came down?"

The shepherdess had put her hands together and, her large eyes fixed for the first time on those of her companion, dispatched an ardent prayer in a whisper.

"Do you know where I saw them come down?" the boy went on. "Not in the sea, as people believe, but out there in the forest. I saw their bronze backs shining in the moonlight; one might have thought them three huge seagulls settling under the wind; I saw them sink down there, in the direction of the pond. If my dream were true, I would know exactly where to find them, the bells! If they sleep somewhere near here, it is not to the fish in the sea that they sing the mass but to the frogs and the minnows."

And the spinner of flax, her gaze lost in the light blue of that beautiful Easter morning, vibrant with sunlight and distant—oh, so distant!—chimes, placed her hand in that of the plowboy and said: "Let's go!"

And they both went into the woods, the sunlit woods, all flowery with primroses and frail anemones, into the woods filled with a kind of green mist, the tender green of nascent leaves; and in the half-light of belated oaks and chestnut trees dotted with shoots, she marveled at the embalmed frost of wild cherries snowing alongside the pink flakes of eglantines in flower; she marveled, her ears straining toward the voice of the bells, comparing in her naïve faith the festival green of the forest to a cathedral of perfumes and dream, ablaze with candles and fuming with incense, and her bare feet hastened happily over the velvet of the mosses, as if for an entry into Paradise. And he, all vibrant with desire at sensing her, all fresh and embalmed in the freshness of the leaves, so close to him, breathed silently, his heart in a vice and his throat dry, and waves of heat rose to his temples on seeing, under her gaping chemise, the curves of a supple white body, circled with brown around the neck; and like a wild beast he was already darting sly glances to the right and the left, emboldened by the solitude, watching out for the opportunity, for the place—a bed of moss or the shadow of a thicket—in order to lay the girl down there and stifle her cries . . . and already the Devil was sniggering in the foliage when, all of a sudden, the bells were heard.

Audeberthe and Aldric stopped abruptly; an immense undulation of bronze filled the forest, inclining everything in its path, the blades of grass as well as the crowns of the trees; three sonorous voices alternated one after another, two bright and joyous voices in combination with another more resonant, and all three sang, launched at full tilt, with anvil vibrations and fanfare, through the fields. A carillon of delight ran aloft over the entire country, and in the implacably pure sky there was a hymn of deliverance, a hosanna of amour to the sun, to nature and to God. Audeberthe and Aldric had fallen to their knees, and the Devil was no longer sniggering in the foliage; the two children had recognized the bells.

They found them floating, like three enormous bronze flowers, on the lukewarm waters of the pond; sticky with mud and verdigris, their metal shone in places, and under the sunlight their black clappers floated, like the huge pistils of an unknown flower, between the water-lentils and the leaves of nenuphars; a storm of harmony rumbled over their passage, and throughout the forest there was an orchestrated music of brass and stringed instruments, of which the ringing of the three floating bells was the canticle and the chant. Audeberthe and Aldric had stopped, gripped, on the edge, hand in hand, both having become purer than in the first days of their childhood, their hearts drowned in happy ecstasy.

The people of the region, having run into the forest at the resounding appeal of the three bronze ladies, found the two of them, their eyes fixed and praying, kneeling amid the osier-beds of the shore. They recognized then that nothing can prevail against the will of the Lord, that Jesus lives in the depths of pure hearts, and that simple folk down here hold in their hands the mysterious power that commands the world; they placed the three rediscovered bells on large carts and brought them to the village with songs and prayers, the remembrance of which had suddenly returned to them.

The bell-tower mute for three centuries resounded by turns with the joyful ringing of masses and baptisms, festival carillons, melancholy knells and the sweetness of the Angelus; the bats abandoned it and its old roof sheltered swallows' nests again. The Bright, the Thunderous and the Argentine rang at full tilt over the marriage of Aldric and Audeberthe, rang even more joyfully over the birth of their children, and wept softly at the Christian hour of their death.

The Devil no longer sniggered in the foliage thereafter, on the roadsides and behind the hedges, in redeemed Malhantôt, and on Easter Sunday the three faithful bells, when people listen to them carefully, spell out in the wind the three brief syllables of the name of Audeberthe.

THE GLOVED HAND

(*L'Écho de Paris*, 28 November 1893)

For M. Edmond de Goncourt[1]

IT was rather late at night after a dinner of men. While avidly emptying sherry sodas, whiskies and other American drinks, the talkers, some sprawling on divans and others crouching on their heels with their backs to heaps of cushions, in more-or-less Oriental poses, had moved on from politics and current affairs through the theater and women to accidents of morphine and ether. The case of Serge Alitof,[2] obliged to quit Paris in order to

1 Edmond de Goncourt (1822-1896) befriended Lorrain when he first moved to Paris, seemingly regarding him as a substitute for his deceased younger brother Jules, and Lorrain became a regular visitor to Goncourt's salon, the "grenier" [loft]. Lorrain expected to be named in Goncourt's will as a member of what became known as the Académie Goncourt, but he was excluded when Goncourt decided to include both of the brothers who shared the pseudonym J.-H. Rosny.

2 A series of episodes published in the *Écho* under the heading *Le Journal de Serge* were run together when reprinted in book form as *Le Buveur d'âmes* (tr. as *The Soul-Drinker*). The character also figures in several of the stories gathered together as *contes d'un buveur*

escape an obsession of animal resemblance emitted for him by every human face had fueled the conversation for a while, and from the monomania of that poor wretch constrained to flee to the Midi before a Paris populated by men with the mouths of wild beasts and women with avian profiles, we had progressed to passing in review all the nervous troubles cited by doctors Charcot and Lombroso, particularly those involving lesions of the encephalum giving birth to curious phenomena.

Naturally, there was discussion of the parts played by heredity and accidental causes; the delicacy of the mental organism is such that an incident of seemingly slight gravity can provoke the most serious disorders. The personality of each individual ended up getting the upper hand in the general conversation, the eight men gathered there having arrived at making one another confidences of the most baroque nature, in feverish and somewhat altered voices. Accompanied by vaguely disquieting gazes and automatic gestures, there was a fearful exchange of personal impressions of the terrors of childhood or youth, and even the recent past.

"For myself," declared Sargine, "after eleven o'clock in summer and nine o'clock in winter, I can't take a cab, or a club carriage. I live in the Avenue de Wagram, near the Place Pereire. Without being very far away, it isn't very close to the center; in order to get back home, I inevitably pass through places that are somewhat solitary; there are, you'll agree, a few avenues that are rather sinister in the November mist; past the Boulevard de Courcelles,

---

d'éther, as one of several alter egos of the author.

the Boulevard Malesherbes has nothing very relaxing about it, and as for the Rue Cardinet . . .

"Well, I prefer returning from the club on foot, even if it's windy or snowing, and I sometimes have as much as fifty or sixty thousand francs on me. I'm well aware that I have my revolver in my pocket, but a bad encounter is still a bad encounter and a fiacre would cut everything short. But there it is: as soon as I'm installed in that accursed wooden box and the coachman sets off through the deserted streets, *crack!* . . . the compass goes awry and an ineradicable idea installs itself obsessively in here." He touched his forehead with his index finger, between the two eyebrows.

"I've tried everything to get rid of it, and the idea isn't in the least cheerful, as you can imagine. No sooner am I rolling through the dark streets than the conviction is established within me that my coachman is masked— and with what a mask! With a colored mask imitating the human face, a false face, the *false face* of a sixteenth-century highwayman, and I believe that I can see his skin under the covering, and the cloth becomes, in my mind, a face of wax or cardboard sheltering the most abominable projects. It's an ignoble prowler that is sitting on the seat; that false face is taking me, off the bridle, toward some horrible ambush. It's only outside the fortifications, in the sinister solitudes of Aubervilliers or Saint-Ouen, that the nightmarish fiacre—that accursed rolling box whose engineered door resists all my efforts, that midnight hearse, whose sealed shutter I cannot lower and whose secret lock I cannot force—will come to a stop, and all my hairs are bristling and all my flesh becomes inert, and

I'm suffocating, strangled by horror, already murdered in imagination, robbed and struck down, left for dead, my skull pulped, on the hard surface of the road.

"The fiacre stops; my anxious coachman jumps down from his seat and opens the door. 'What's the matter, my bourgeois? Has one fallen asleep?' I see that I'm in my street, outside the door of my house, and, still shivering, I'm only too glad to give a five-franc tip to my bewildered driver.

"You understand now why I go home on foot."

And before a unanimous smile, Sargine, in his slack voice, went on: "And all that for having taken, one evening of Mardi Gras, without perceiving it, a coachman with a false nose, a poor inoffensive fellow who had put on the traditional cardboard red nose in order to celebrate the carnival; there was an accident, he broke a trace; to repair it would take five minutes and he thought he ought to warn me. I was half-asleep, I opened my eyes and I saw that mask before me, that frightful artifice, at one o'clock in the morning, in the Avenue de Villars, behind the Invalides, where I had promised to go to a ball to meet one of my blonde friends for the cotillion.

"You can imagine the scene. It was cold enough to crack stones that night, with a bright moon, exceedingly bright, in a sky traversed by inky clouds. I thought it was a nocturnal attack and fell upon the man with arms raised.

"But ever since—it's stronger than me—I can't take a cab."

To which Martimpré countered: "A fiacre after midnight—that's certainly a state of mind often generated by

75

my nocturnal excursions, as I live in Auteuil[1] and I don't want, under any pretext, to return by train—because for me, its something else; it's in a first-class compartment . . . or a second-class, but a first-class most of all . . . where I become unhinged and go literally mad as soon as the lamps are lit! And the twelve-forty train, the theater train, how often I had taken it, and how often I had loved and blessed it before my little adventure three years ago! Oh, I had used it frequently, the little trick of all the inhabitants of Neuilly, Passy and Auteuil, which consists of hurling oneself into a fiacre at twenty past midnight in order to be in the waiting room at twelve forty and in the Boulevard Montmorency, at the terminus of the last train, at ten past one. That little half hour on the train is a little more reassuring, all the same, than a solo trip in the coffin of a fiacre through the equivocal steppes of the Avenue de Versailles, with its shady mariners' and vagabonds' inns, with closed shutters but windows still ablaze at one o'clock and two o'clock in the morning.

"Yes, it simplified my existence for at least ten years, that good railway adored by suburbans, but now, for three years . . . no, no, stop laughing . . . I prefer to shiver in my furs in the middle of winter, my feet rigid on the ever-icy foot-warmer of a nocturnal fiacre . . . and yet I'm not, myself, an etheromaniac like Alitof or a dotard like Sargine . . ."

---

1 Lorrain moved to Auteuil in the early 1890s from an apartment in the Rue de Courty, to which he frequently referred as his "haunted house" because of the ether-induced hallucinations he had suffered there while writing late at night.

The latter bowed as a sign of thanks, and Martimpré sank even further in his Hungarian needlepoint armchair, crossed his legs, and continued in his habitual nonchalant tone:

"This was my little adventure. Before commencing, you'll grant me that there's nothing more impressive and, I dare say, nothing more macabre than the lighting in the first-class compartments on the Western line. It becomes terrible, with a brutality that emphasizes all the features while deforming them. It's simultaneously reminiscent of the reflector at the Morgue and the diffuse lighting of an amphitheater. All visages take on a deathly pallor, the eyes are hollowed out under the exaggerated relief of the eyelids, the nostrils fill with shadow, and in the faces, which have all become death's heads under the luminous flood of the lamps, most of the mouths resemble black holes. The slightest cavity or projection of bone or muscle takes on a disquieting relief, and, no matter how little the physique of the traveler lends itself to it, you can easily believe without any great effort of imagination that you are in a hospital ward, in the company of invalids in a bad way, or even choice corpses in a dissecting hall."

One of the listeners having said: "Charming. But a trifle long, that little prayer to the dying," Martimpré smiled complaisantly, uncrossed his right leg, which he had placed over the left, resumed the same position in reverse, and went on: "I see that it's agreed. You concede me the spectral and truly horrible aspect of the lighting of our railway carriages, so I'll get to the point.

"It was three years ago. I came out of the Porte-Saint-Martin, where I had seen one of the last performances of *Cléopâtre*.[1] Oh, the Botticelli that was evoked then by the divine Sarah in her envelopes of lamé fabric, fastened here and there by turquoise scarabs and Egyptian jewelry. Never had her resemblance to the Primavera of the famous Florentine fresco been so preciously emphatic, and in spite of my scant taste for Sardou's drama, it was the tenth or eleventh time that I had seen it, attracted by the unforgettable plastic vision offered by the tragedienne.

"If I insist thus on the spectacle from which I was emerging, it's in order to mark for you my state of mind that evening, not at all turned to black thoughts—entirely to the contrary, since a delightful image of art was still floating, as if alive, in my memory. I climbed into a carriage, therefore, that filled up almost immediately—the compartments of the last train always fill up rapidly—and we departed. I had not even looked at the seven traveling companions that hazard had given me. There is always a profusion of furs on the part of the men and a considerable number of shiny pelisses and brooches on the part of the women in that so-called theater train, and the public, cravated in white, brightly gloved and all bejeweled, is rather elegant—polished, even. At any rate, I was not paying much attention to them as we rolled along, and at each station—Courcelles, Neuilly, Bois-de-Boulogne—couples descended from the compartment, which gradually emptied.

---

1 The title-role in *Cléopâtre* by Victorien Sardou and Emile Moreau, was one of Sarah Bernhardt's greatest triumphs, performed in Paris and elsewhere on numerous occasions between 1890 and 1896. Lorrain made continual references to it in his reviews and critical articles.

"By the Trocadéro I remained alone, and it was then that I noticed another traveler dozing in a corner almost opposite me, leaning on the movable intermediate elbow-rest. Small, with high shoulders that seemed to rise above his ears, the sleeping man displayed under the brutal light of the lamp the most frightful ugliness: a large pear-shaped head, wider at the bottom than the top, a prognathous face with terrible maxillae, a narrow and low forehead devoured by shiny black hair, an olive complexion with heavy, fat and lazy eyelids, a short, flat nose, and, within its green-tinted pallor, the tumefied pads of two thick, hideously slack lips; one of those nightmarish faces that Goya lends to his scenes of *comprachictos*,[1] and which the museum of Madrid presents in the portraits of the last Hapsburgs—the ugliness of the degeneracy of a great family descended to the murderous ferocity of the brute.

"I gazed at the man; he had a frightful fashion of sleeping; his thick eyelids did not meet, and a little of the whites of his eyes could be seen in the gaps; one might have thought that his gaze was lying in ambush behind the grilles of his eyelashes, and although he was snoring, as if to reassure me with I know not what hideous rattle in the depths of his throat, he was resting on his knees a long hand gloved in black, a hand simultaneously clenched and inert, immeasurably long and insanely narrow, which seemed poorly accommodated in the white cuff of his shirt, and surely could not be the hand of his body.

"That became an obsession; I could no longer take my eyes off that hand. Suddenly, the man stood up—it

---

1 The famous series of prints in question is actually titled *Los Caprichos*.

was after Passy station and the train had just moved off again—took a few steps within the carriage and came to plant himself in front of me. It was frightful. His thick eyelids were raised and his white eyes were staring at me; the man had put his hands into his pocket, and, both arms plunged to the elbows in his overcoat, he searched me with his vitreous gaze without saying a word, and I understood then that he was still asleep.

"Five minutes of unforgettable anguish followed, face to face with that strange somnambulist, in the silence and the trepidation of that night train! We arrived in the Auteuil station; the application of the brakes caused my companion to totter on his short legs and he nearly fell; he grunted and bore both hands to his eyes, and, as if suddenly recalled to a notion of things, he headed for a door in order to descend on to the parallel track.

"Maneuvers were being carried out there, and, finally reassured, I thought I ought to warn him. 'Not that way, not that way,' I said, touching his arm. He stifled another grunt and, without responding to me, threw himself through the other open door and descended into the void. He had disappeared . . .

"A singular traveler! I was about to get down in my turn when my foot collided with something soft and I bent down in order to see what it was. I found beneath my fingers the hand, the horrible gloved hand, immeasurably long and insanely narrow, a hand already cold, inert and clenched, which the somnambulist had forgotten.

"It was a woman's hand—freshly severed, for it was still oozing and had left red patches on the cushions."

And Martimpré added, in his languid tone: "That's why I never took the twelve-forty train again."

TALES OF ENCHANTMENT
(*L'Écho de Paris*, 15 December 1893)

For Antonio de La Gandara[1]

U NDER the rigid gray skies of December, while passers-by rendered ugly by the cold hasten and bump into one another at street-corners and the north wind torments with its feline ferocities the ragged individuals lingering on the white surface of the roads, how pleasant it would be to be able to go back into the past, to become a child again, huddled beside red embers in the warmth of a closed room, and how relaxing and refreshing it would be to poor eyes worn away by life to be recaptured by the images of old illustrated books and to believe once again in old tales.

In an atmosphere of magic and dream, those tales of enchantment, which have been replaced today by accounts of voyages and scientific discoveries, were marvel-

---

1 The painter Antonio de La Gandara (1861-1917) was one of Lorrain's closest friends in café society, and Lorrain commissioned him to paint a portrait of his mother when she came to live with him in Auteuil.

81

ous stories that spoke to the heart via the imagination and prepared pity by means of ingenious motifs of compassion for chimerical princesses, delighted and dazzled my quivering young soul in the early years of my childhood. How sorry I feel deep within myself for the children of the present generation, who read Jules Verne instead of Perrault and Flammarion instead of Andersen! The practical families of those children do not know what kind of youth they are preparing for all those bicycle-riders. It is not in the world of slightly delicate emotion that the love of the marvelous resides; the soul of a landscape is entirely in the more-or-less populous memory of the voyager who traverses it; there are no mountains, forests, sunrises over glaciers or sunsets over lakes from which one does not simultaneously desire and dread to see Oriane emerge from the edge of a wood, Tiphaine in the midst of the furze or Melusine from a spring.

Who, ignorant of Homer, Theocritus and Sophocles, could really desire to visit Sicily and Greece? And in order to love the vast cup of liquid sapphire that is the Mediterranean with the delicate amour that Paul Arène[1] brings to it, is it not necessary to have heard a little more than the song of the cicadas in the olive groves around the farms, and a little more than the cries of Provençal mariners in the rigging? It is the memory of Parthenope that makes the Bay of Naples intoxicating, and, if the Mediterranean sees so many indifferent and skeptical

---

1 Paul Arène (1843-1896) was another member of the stable assembled by Catulle Mendès to supply the *Écho* with material on a near-weekly basis; like Lorrain he mingled occasional fantasies with his many naturalistic stories and travelogues.

people returning to its seaside resorts every winter, it is because the transparent azure of its waves once caressed and rolled in their breakers the white bodies of the Sirens.

It is necessary, then, to love tales of enchantment and the places from which they come: Greece and Norway, Swabia or Spain, Bretagne or the Orient. They are the flowering almond-trees of youthful imaginations; the wind carries away their petals and life disseminates the dream, but something remains in spite of that to bear fruit, and that fruit perfumes the whole autumn. Whoever has not believed as a child will not dream as a young man; it is necessary to think, on the very threshold of life, of weaving beautiful tapestries of dream in order to ornament our shelter for the approach of winter, and beautiful dreams, even when faded, make the sumptuous tapestries of December.

It is necessary, therefore, to love tales of enchantment; it is necessary to nourish ourselves on them and intoxicate ourselves with them, like a light and slightly dangerous wine, but whose bitter savor, without artificial sweetening, is insistent and persistent—and it is that savor which, when the meal is finished, enchants the palate and sometimes permits a sickened guest to remain at the table.

For myself, I confess, I have adored, with an almost savage adoration, tales that are proscribed and disdained today; they were misty tales of the North, steeped in moonlight and rain sown with snowflakes, for I only discovered later in life the enchantment of the sunlit life of the Midi. It was on the shore of the turbulent glaucous Atlantic, perpetually striped with surf, in a small coastal town besieged by the west wind, that I spent my entire childhood. As early as November there was nothing but squalls and storms, and during the night, heavy packets of seawater ran along the jetties with the sinister *hou, hou, hou* of giant seagulls. In the tales brought to us by bearded matelots sheathed to mid-thigh in streaming boots, reeking like them of cold, mist, melted snow, tar and the sea, there was more question of auroral nights and moonlit shipwrecks than of cheerful rides in bright mornings, but I adored their melancholy, in which a slightly naïve marvelous made of hope and distress fluttered, as if skimming the waves: a poetry of the simple soul terrified by the blind fury of the elements but tenderized by nostalgia, and sustained in spite of everything by faith in return.

Then too, those hallucinatory tales, whose characters galloped all night in my curtains, signaled the return of the Newfoundlanders to port, the return of the men to their homes, and joy throughout the town. It was the moment of continual evening meetings, visits from one house to another through ill-lit streets, the season of long evenings spent by the hearth before bowls of warm cider, fresh cider that was mixed with cinnamon while guzzling chestnuts—and what fine stories were told on those evenings!

In our house, that happened in the kitchen; the cook always had a Newfoundlander son or a husband, the chambermaid a brother, a cousin or a suitor who traveled to Iceland, and once the work was finished, it was almost an established custom in the bourgeoisie of the town to save a place by the fireside for relatives of the maidservants during the first month of their sojourn on land—

and there was scarcely more than that, for they were at sea for nine months, poor fellows, and many stayed away even longer.

In the drawing room, the captain of the ship was received, along with the associate ship-owner and the directors of insurance companies who had arrived after some disaster; and while the men talked business, some pretty hand tightened at the wrist with a gold bracelet leafed indolently through the illustrated pages of a volume of tales, tales of enchantment, the images of which a soft female voice explained to us—for we were approaching New Year's Day and the season of gifts was commencing. How I preferred to the hard-bound books with gilt-edges, with their beautiful plates, though, the tales told aloud in the kitchen by men in reefer jackets and berets, in the midst of trembling maidservants. Their stories seemed to me to be truer, born of a fantasy both more distant and more alive, and among those seamen's stories, one above all enchanted me: a nostalgic and thrilling tale of the North which I found later in Andersen but which, in the mouths of those rude Newfoundlanders, took on the savage intensity of something encountered and lived, for they had certainly crossed the path in unquiet seas, in the course of their perilous journeys, of the pale Snow Queen, the memory of whom still obsesses and captivates me.[1]

---

1 The remainder of this article reprinted, with slight modifications, a brief essay entitled "La Reine des neiges" [The Snow Queen], dedicated to Edmond de Goncourt, first published the previous year under the signature Raitif de la Bretonne, in a series headed *Fleurs de rêve* [Flowers of Dream] in the *Écho* of 14 December 1892. Lorrain subsequently wrote a Christmas tale of his own based on

It happened in a distant and populous town in Norway, resounding with the cries and whip-cracks of conductors of sleighs; warmly-wrapped children played there all day long in the main square, and in the narrow streets of the outlying districts, so narrow that the poor people in the mansards went to visit one another by means of bridges of planks extended between the houses. Snowflakes fell silently for six months of the year out of twelve, speckling the gray sky like a mobile ermine cloak.

There, in the old tall house of an artisan, with small windows whose sills were florid in June with sweet peas and nasturtiums, lived a worthy grandmother with a quavering voice whom in the bleak days of winter, distaff in hand, recounted legends to two little children crouched at her feet before a hearth, who already loved one another amorously.

Outside, the white swarm of snowflakes fluttered in the mute air, ever more dense; and the tales of the old grandmother called those flakes white bees, saying that those white bees had a queen, like the golden bees of summer, but that she was a queen entirely made of ice, with two frozen moonbeams on her shoulders by way of wings, and a long cloak of frost fringed with snowy fog. Her hive was beyond the pole, beneath the Arctic skies swarming with stars, and there was a bleak moonless palace constructed of ice-floes, icicles and icebergs, all pallor and splendor: an enormous, spectral palace with vast deserted halls swept day and night by the north wind,

the Hans Christian Andersen story of the Snow Queen, "Neighilde" (*Le Journal* 27 December 1898; tr. in *Masks in the Tapestry*).

with dazzling and rigid transparent cupolas, eternally set ablaze by the aurora borealis.

Oh, that Snow Queen, standing in the immense redness of that eternally empty palace! How I loved her and feared her at the same time, that queen of the winter bees petrified by lethargy, that august virgin of the livid visions of the pole! For the hoarse voice of the grandmother of the tale also made her a wanderer and traveler, and on December nights, it could happen, while gazing at the sky, that one saw the icy sleigh of the queen there. Like a dot in the midst of the clouds, it flew rapidly above towns, straits and seas; great flocks of frightened geese fled before it, and sailors on watch, leaning on the rail, made the sign of the cross repeatedly on seeing the rigid white spur of the royal sleigh pass through the fine rigging.

Oh, that Snow Queen, with her cenacle of old wolves sitting in a circle on the edges of fjords, howling mortally, with what a delectable anguish and poignant terror she filled my childish soul!

In my terrified imagination I saw her passing, impassive, high in the sky, in the midst of a white turbulence of bees, with enormous black crows fluttering around her, crying famine and crying winter; over her shoulders a vast cloak of moonlight floated, immeasurably long in the night, and for me, during hard frosts, it is always her who comes to draw on the windows with her rigid fingertips the great eccentric flowers and arborescences of frost. And I have always been afraid, at midnight, of seeing surge forth from the panes of my window, the extinct eyes and luminous face of the dormant queen, for I have listened attentively to the legends and I know that when the Snow Queen looks at you, her soul is elsewhere and her eyes do not see you; she is far away, far beyond the Arctic Ocean, in the polar ice-cap, out there, far beyond the straits and seas,

> *In the eternal palace of ice*
> *Where future winters are asleep.*

FAIRY LAND

ILSE

(*L'Echo de Paris*, 6 July 1894)

ILSE was born in the land of the fays, but did not live there; in order to be born in that chimerical country it is sufficient to have a vivid and tender imagination and a very pure soul, and that was true of Ilse. Being very pure, Ilse was very pious, but she had a strange religion, a little girl's religion that made her believe as firmly in the Holy Virgin as in fays, kobolds and dwarves; she also believed in elves and thought that flowers have souls; she knew very well that the Holy Virgin loves flowers; because of that she carried a sunflower every Saturday to the little painted statuette at the corner of the Kreuzstrasse.

She spoke in a familiar way to little Jesus, as she spoke to the bullfinch in his cage and the flowers in her garden; she believed in paradise and in the land of the fays, but she never thought about Hell.

Ilse lived in Bamberg, a city of old houses with a picturesque border as dentellate as those in an etching by Whistler, and among those strange dwellings, the strangest was her own, a narrow little house, entirely black, with a little black roof advancing over a balcony that also protruded; the waters of the river Mein ran at the foot and bathed a thin line of soil where the immense sunflowers grew. Their yellow heads rose up almost as far as the balcony, and the minuscule windows of the little house were only slightly larger than the flowers.

Ilse was seven years old; she lived with her brother, Hans Turner, a handsome fellow as brown as a ribeira-dweller,[1] who had been married for four years to Kathrine, the daughter of a neighbor, Peret, and had a little child baptized Richard, because of Wagner, whose glory made the fortune of the region.

Ilse, Hans Turner and Kathrine lived on the right bank of the river, at the edge of the town, and the silhouette of the Rathaus closed their horizon.

Hans Turner was a fisherman and sailed for long days on the Mein, and for long nights too. Hans Turner did not demand any work from Ilse, because he was very proud of her delicate beauty. Kathrine was sufficient for the work of the household, so Ilse had nothing to do except to guard the little child sometimes and care for the bullfinch, which lived in a cage near the window like a pomegranate flower on a wall. She also occupied herself with the large sunflowers.

Ilse was happy. She never had any chagrin, and the idea that she might be unhappy never occurred to her. Everyone loved her, and she loved everyone, for Ilse was

---

1 Ribeira is Portuguese for river, and the term is employed as a proper name for numerous districts in various regions of countries where that language is spoken.

very pretty, with eyes as blue as veronicas and hair as golden as sunflowers; she was as pale as white convolvulus, tall, thin and supple; she resembled a little princess. Ilse had a peaceful and simple life, which went by as uniformly and untroubled as the river before her house. Who could believe that this delightful illustration in stained-glass, which one might think copied from a Holbein of Bâle, this periwinkle soul of an Andersen heroine, whose brief story, as dolorous and predictable as the eternal adventure of his sister Gretchen, has the distant grace of legend, could have bloomed in the hothouse of a mundane existence? And yet, that was the case; the author, who dissimulates herself under the pseudonym Ossit[1] and published twelve years ago the most curious art criticism that we have in France of the painter Burne-Jones, is, it would be pleasant to believe, a woman of the

---

1 "Ossit" was the pseudonym of Madeleine Vivier-Deslandes (1866-1929), who had briefly been the Comtesse de Fleury following a disastrous arranged marriage that was annulled by the Vatican. She lived thereafter in Paris, where she hosted a notable literary salon; she travelled to England in 1893 to meet Edward Burne-Jones, about whom she was writing an article; he painted her portrait, completed in 1896, after the present story was published. *Ilse* (1894) was the second of her four pseudonymous novels, which received no great publicity in France apart from the present paean. Several sources report that she once recited a poem by Jean Richepin in a lion's cage, but the anecdote was spread—and surely invented—by Robert de Montesquiou, who was notoriously catty in his comments on female writers. Lorrain's disciple and imitator Delphi Fabrice credited a similar publicity stunt to the pretentious poet Jean des Glaïeuls, a character reminiscent of the flamboyant image that Lorrain adopted after the turn of the century, and Lorrain was once assaulted after an unkind review by the dancer "Bob Walter," who really did perform a version of Loie Fuller's "serpentine dance" in a cage with four lions.

world, and one of the noblest by birth. For what we know of her, thanks to that anonymous socialite, whose presence and corsage excite at suburban dinners, as pastels and portraits do at inaugurations of salons, and for what we know by virtue of loving the beautiful mysterious and golden legends of Germany and Norway, the tales of Andersen quivering with an immense pity and such a pensive philosophy beneath their child-like appearance, we congratulate her sincerely, as it would have been so facile to be simply an exquisite wearer of the mauve and green dresses that Burne-Jones was glad to design for her. What we felicitate and compliment her for is for having wanted to have a little of the soul of tales of enchantment for proving it to us by giving us today this childish and touching story of Ilse, which seems to be written with tears and with dew, the tears of flowers!

To the mayoral gods of little Ilse, aged seventeen years, who was loved for three days in Bamberg, on the bank of the Mein, and died. Such is the very epitaph of the book, for Ilse, naturally, has to love and die. To that soul of a little princess blooming in a poor fisherman's dwelling and prosaically betrothed to a good dim-witted neighbor—worse than that, a grocer—the river was to bring one day, as the Escaut once brought Lohengrin to the anguish of Elsa, the daughter of the king, the implored prince of legend dreamed of by all little Ilses with eyes the color of veronicas and hair the color of the sun.

The portrait that Ossit traces is, in any case, conclusive; the future murderer of Ilse is a dilettante and an idler, one smitten with sensations, but also fatigued.

He was a spectator; he loved the arts passionately, but he did not practice any with any success whatsoever, although that was because of his extreme nonchalance and his versatility rather than any lack of natural talent.

He was very handsome and very spoiled, but that did not content him. He had a melancholy soul, enthusiastic but disabused; he was not capable of any sustained effort, or any consequence in his ideas; he was not good and he was not wicked, he was merely an idler. He drifted through life, and understood his futility.

That type of disgusted voyager, weary and discontented, we have already encountered in Bourget and elsewhere, but what does it matter? He arrives so appropriately in old Bamberg with the Whistlerian houses, that handsome Italian prince—and slightly Irish via his mother—returning from performances at Bayreuth! The aspect of Bamberg charms him; he stays there for a day, in order to make a sketch of the Rathaus, leaning on the bridge in order to get a better view of it; he spots a flat-bottomed boat, hails the men manning it, embarks, goes down river, and before a black house between two hedges of yellow suns, he stops, dazzled, fully satisfied in all his artistic senses by the appearance of a young woman in a blue *vergissmeinnicht* dress[1] standing with a pink-clad infant in her arms: Ilse herself, radiant in her almost chimerical beauty, amid the water and the flowers.

To be smitten with her as with an ornament, to respire her as one respires a rose, to amuse himself with that credulous and legendary little soul without loving

---

1 *Vergissmeinnicht* is the German name of the flower known in English—by virtue of a literal translation—as the forget-me-not.

her, without desiring her, to make a game of taking possession of that soul and imprinting the memory of him upon it forever: all of that cruel maneuver appeared to the handsome de Trevi to be a restful and fresh summer relaxation.

Never to be forgotten, to remain the secret hope of a soul until its final hour, the dilettante that de Trevi was could not resist; he closed his heart to pity and with all the Italian grace and dangerous charm of his race he collected in three days all the dreams and all the life of that poor little Ilse, who died of it.

We have witnessed that cruel shredding of a soul before in *On ne badine pas avec l'amour*,[1] but the Perdican of Alfred de Musset is not the pitiless murderer that Ossit's hero is; Perdican kills the soul of Rosette and her poor body unconsciously; in his egoistic passion for Camille, simultaneously exasperated and driven to despair by that proud girl depraved by the nuns, he tries to irritate her pride by pretending to love the little village girl; he does not suppose for an instant that it will cost his victim her life. *One does not trifle with amour*: in Musset the death of Rosette is homicide by imprudence. In Ossit's romance, by contrast, de Trevi is a veritable malefactor, a poisoner of the Borgia stripe, who kills out of curiosity, for love of the art, almost a moral and immoral surgeon of amour.

And de Trevi is all the more without excuse because he is conscious of his work and pitied by his victim. Ossit has placed in the cathedral of Bamberg perhaps the most

---

1 The text of Alfred de Musset's play *On ne badine pas avec amour* was published in 1834 in the *Revue des Deux Mondes*, but it was not produced until 1861, at the Comédie française.

touching scene in her book, for there is a cathedral, naturally, in this golden legend of sorts, and in that cathedral a statue of Conrad III, which plays a strange and eccentric role.

On the eve of his departure, Ilse has taken her adored prince into the Dom. She has taken him to admire the statue of her emperor—her protector, as she calls him—for she believes in the protection of statues as she believes in that of angels, the Holy Virgin and the queen of the fays; the child's sense of security has ignited in the handsome de Trevi the evil desire to take her and to doom her, for Ilse's confidence has touched his heart like a challenge. The cruel dilettante that Brian de Trevi is takes her that very evening, therefore, in one of their pensive strolls along the river; he has just decided that in his heart; what does it matter if the child dies of it? And here they are, emerging from the cathedral, if I may be permitted here to quote:

Before leaving, Ilse knelt down—without shame or ostentation, very simply, because it was her custom—and with her bright eyes upraised she prayed.

He remained standing beside her, his hat in his hand, slightly moved.

Then they left the church.

Stopping suddenly, he asked: "Ilse, for what have you just been praying?"

The little white face went pink. "I was praying to God that you would always be happy," she said, simply, "and I thanked him for the great joy of having known you."

Something in her words touched him. Rapidly, he took her hands between his, and gravely pressed his lips to them.

95

'If there is a God somewhere,' he thought, 'this little girl is close to his heart,' and silently, while she was speaking, he took her home.

"I'm departing tomorrow," he said. "I want to leave you tranquil." He promised, however, to come and fetch her in the evening, in order to go out on the water, because the moon would be bright.

For that minute of tenderness, the dilettante Brian respected the virgin physically, but he had already captured the poor little chimerical and quivering soul of Ilse, who, for having strolled three times in the moonlight with a handsome stranger, would die with despair in her heart—which proves that beautiful souls are like butterflies, flowers and birds, brief, pretty and futile things; that it is dangerous to be a frail being down here, as pure and as beautiful as a symbol; and that a soul of crystal always breaks.

THE FIELD OF PANSIES

(*L'Écho de Paris*, 10 August 1894; reprinted in *Le Journal*, 11 April 1896 as "Récit du moine" [The Monk's Tale])

PRINCE OLAF was sixteen years old. He had grown up in fasting and prayer in the meditative shadow of a cloister. Olaf was the son of the king, but the monks were ignorant of his birth. Murders, rapes and tortures had bloodied the palace of his ancestors; his father had been murdered on the orders of his two brothers, but the devotion of an old servant had saved the infant from the massacre; the man had thrown the frightened young prince on to a horse and, fleeing at a gallop from the burning city, where the partisans were still battling, he had covered sixty leagues of plains and valleys in three days in order to come and fall, exhausted—he, the horse and the child—on the threshold of the old monastery lost in the Pyrenees. The horse had not got up again, the man had died within a week, of a wound inflicted by an arrow as he fled; as for the royal orphan, the cloister had taken him in.

Sitting in the light of a narrow window, clad in an ample white woolen robe, in which his robust frame seemed slender, all day long he painted delicate ornamental and heraldic trefoils copied from the margins of antique missals: delightful arabesque fleurons with nascent dreamlike calices, decorated with gold and azure, blossoming on the slightly yellowed ivory of old parchments.

He followed the monks to matins, sometimes serving the officiating father during mass, and in the twilight of summer evenings he lingered with the other novices listening to some Bohemian, tolerated for a night within the enclosure of the convent, telling stories—but that was a rare distraction; it was rare for the companions of the "gay science" to pass through the abrupt gorges and high fir-woods, where the rumbling plaint of eternal torrents sounded. A cold shadow falling from the mountains weighed upon the narrow valley like a mantle of ice, and sparkling snows on steely summits closed the horizon.

It was a grim retreat, steep and sure, and the outlaw childhood of the fallen little king flourished there unconsciously, fervent and calm, like a beautiful royal lily, in the obscure cell of a centenarian monk, sheltered from the rumors and dangers of the world. His uncles, the usurpers, continued battling, and, gnawed by ambition and criminal covetousness, continued to agitate and desolate the realm with their wretched dissensions; the blood that was shed had summoned blood, and the two thieves of the crown, the two fratricidal kings, were now disputing the pitiful land that had fallen into their hands by means of iron and fire, through all kinds of traps, ambushes and surprise attacks.

Did God take pity one day on that sad people, torn and bloody in the claws of vultures? After ten years of intestinal struggles, unexpected and almost simultaneous palace tragedies delivered the land. The elder of the tyrants, Frédégaire,[1] was poisoned by one of his vassals in Béziers, besieged for three months by his younger brother Merewild. Merewild, attained by fevers that had been ravaging his camp since the autumn rains, was carried off twenty-four hours after Frédégaire's tragic end, at the moment when, delighted by the sinister news, he was rejoicing on his deathbed and giving the order to deliver an assault.

And there was deadlight throughout the land; the funeral knell rang again in the cathedrals where the people were intoning *Te Deums*. Processions of peasants—men, women and children—filed through the valleys, their foreheads crowned with primroses, toward humble rural madonnas, some preceded by deacons, others by simple clerics, all intending to offer thanks to Our Lady of Alms and Succor, who had finally taken pity on them, and great bonfires of joy were lit on the mountains.

Leaning on the sill of the little window of his cell, the melancholy novice Olaf watched them burn; he knew that the two kings, of a kingdom that extended from Aquitaine into Spain, were dead—a goatherd had brought him the news four days ago—but what did those two ferocious kings matter to him? The two

---

1 The name Frédégaire is taken from an assembly of Merovingian manuscripts apparently originating from the seventh century, collectively known in English as the Chronicle of Fredegar. There is no mention therein of a brother named Merewild.

bloody soldiers that he had never known, and their atrocious struggles with iron and poison that he would never know, were irrelevant to him, a soul as innocent as the lamb or the Lord, raised in monastic shade and destined for the cloister.

The news had, however, excited, more profoundly than one might think, the superior of the community. Two monks had departed immediately on missions, one to the Archbishop of Burgos and the other to the Archbishop of Pampeluna. Four days had already gone by, and for four days fires had burned every evening partway up the sides of the encircling mountains, setting the snow of the glaciers ablaze; and for four days, a feverish impatience racked the whole convent, where the young Olaf sensed an unaccustomed deference and a respectful and caressant benevolence rising around him.

And as he watched the snow of the surrounding peaks turning pink and crimson in the gathering night, the sound of little bells and whinnying caused him to lean out of the window and discover a file of caparisoned mules mounted by monks. He had never seen them before; some of them were wearing shiny dalmatics whose golden thread gleamed and glinted, reflecting the light of the fires lit on the mountains; breastplates scintillated around a frail old man, seemingly crushed by a miter, and hurrahs rose from the valley all the way to the walls of the calm monastery, suddenly filled with fearful whispers and footfalls.

Then, a great silence suddenly fell; the cortege had entered the convent. The sound of sandals trailed for a few minutes along the corridors, and then the monastery became as mute as a tomb; all the monks had gone downstairs, summoned to the chapter, at eight o'clock in the evening, the customary hour of prayer! And the intrigued novice listened at his door, uncomprehendingly.

Suddenly, the heavy batten opened. It was the superior himself, even calmer and graver than usual, with infinitely sad eyes. Without even appearing to notice the curiosity of the young monk, he gave Olaf an order to follow him. They both descended into the courtyard. All the monks of the convent were assembled there, bare-headed with arms folded, around a frail and tottering old man coiffed with a miter: a bishop. Grim helmeted figures were holding up flaming torches, for the fires on the mountains were beginning to go out, and golden copes were shining strangely here and there in the crowd.

"Bless him, Father, and may your benediction inspire him!"

The superior, having pushed the bewildered Olaf under the extended hands of the bishop, took him almost immediately thereafter to two saddled and bridled horses. The superior bestrode one and Olaf mounted the other; and the novice and the abbot passed through the abbatial porch into open country, to the sound of psalms intoned by the monks.

They rode for a long time through the mountains; valleys succeeded one another, torrents precipitated from the heights with a sound like breaking glass, and they sometimes went along narrow goat-paths overhanging abysms from which a sepulchral breath rose. The fires on the hillsides had been extinct for a long time and their mounts sometimes stumbled; stones could be heard falling and rolling into the gulfs, but the superior remained silent.

The rising moon eventually illuminated the land-scape; a silver sheet bathed the entire horizon and the summits of glaciers appeared, like frost, against the cold blue of the sky. The superior drew his mount closer to Olaf's, and began to speak. He told him about his birth, the iniquitous and bloody death of his father, the atrocious exploits of his uncles and all the sins of his family; the reigns of twenty kings aggrandized by frauds, treasons, murders and massacres; the ephemeral power of twenty pillaged crowns snatched from the distress, tears, blood and famine of a people, a sacrilegious power, recognized nevertheless, of which the death of the last two kings of his race had made him the heir.

Utterly pale in the moonlight, the novice listened. They had arrived before an immense field situated high in the mountains and descending in a gentle slope toward a small lake misted by vapors. A circle of glaciers surrounded it, and in the white lunar light, the immense sloping meadow was sleeping peacefully, every tuft of grass enameled and dotted with little wild pansies: singular little yellow and black pansies, which the moonlight caused to appear as white velvet.[1]

The superior stopped. "The first of your race, Alaric,[2]

---

1 The French *pensées* [pansies] also means "thoughts"—an ambiguity fundamental to the symbolism of the flower in question in *fin-de-siècle* fantasy, in which pansies often grow on ground sown with corpses, as, for instance, in Georges de Peyrebrune's "Salomé" (*L'Écho de Paris*, 27 December 1889).

2 "Alaric the Goth," credited with taking part in the sack of Rome in 410, had previously been allied with the Romans against the Franks, and is generally believed to have been born in the Balkans, but Merovingian legendry was rather promiscuous in its adoptions from history.

a simple adventurer from the marches of Aquitaine, traversed this field three hundred years ago. It was on a clear night like this one. Two ancient kings, of whom legend has lost even the names, two enemy brothers like your uncles, had fought a battle here—a futile battle, since they killed one another therein—but the lunar meadow was entirely white with bones, which the earth has devoured since. The carcasses of horses and men strewed the funeral grassland everywhere; but on one human skull, already green-tinted and corroded by moss, a golden circle gleamed in the darkness. Alaric, your ancestor, dismounted and bent down to pick it up, but the horse's hoof had collided with the cranium and the sniggering skull rolled into the lake, taking the crown with it.

"Alaric dived into the water of the lake, seized the circlet and, having returned to the shore, placed the crown on his head, saying: 'I shall be king.' And he was,

"Prince Olaf, think about all the dead who are asleep under this soil, think about the crimes of your family, the murders of the past, and the death of your father, and respond as to whether you want to be king, like him."

"Let us return to the convent," replied the novice.

"The convent? You are renouncing royalty?"

"Let us return to the convent to pray for them, and never emerge again."

THE FROG PRINCE

(*L'Écho de Paris* 2 October 1894; reprinted in *Le Journal* 7 August 1898)

A Tale after Walter Crane[1]

IN a garden planted with orange trees and cypresses, Princess Sylviane is sitting. Her yellow brocade dress strewn with rusty chrysanthemums over a backcloth of narcissi with golden hearts, tapers and broadens in long pleats around her; her vaguely astonished eyes are the color of violets; they are violently widened, and a little silver crown fixes a thin reflection of moonlight in her auburn hair.

Princess Silviane is sixteen years old; she is the daughter of the King. The tall hornbeams of a royal park and lawns where the ocellated tails of peacocks surround her with a décor of verdant foliage dappled with enamel

---

1 Walter Crane (1845-1915) was the most prolific and enterprising illustrator of books of children's tales in the last quarter of the nineteenth century. The famous series beginning with *The Frog Prince* (1874) was influenced by Japanese art, which also exerted a strong influence on French "decadent" artists such as Odilon Redon.

rose-windows. Twelve steps of black marble descend into the water of a large pond; a spring aliments it with liquid falling back from a bronze bowl, moving cyprinoids animate its silky surface, and the princess comes here to dream during the heat of the day. A semicircular marble bench receives her between two faience lions with eyes of phosphorescent shadow.

That is her favorite place of retreat.

"Oh, how pretty you will be, dear soul, as Princess Silviane," interjected Maud Beecocosme, casting an arm as fresh as milk around Miss Lily's neck. "I have a new blue pencil that Charley has just sent me from London; I'll lend it to you in order to magnify your eyes; but where will we find the dress sown with rusty chrysanthemums against a background of golden narcissi?"[1]

To which Miss Lily replied: "Don't worry, my darling, I've seen delightful fabric designs at Liberty."

"Oh, Liberty! What horror! It is, as the French say, London's Bon Marché; one can only go to Chez Morice."

"We'll go to Chez Morice, then, but let's finish reading the story. It's necessary not to doubt it for a minute longer, my beloved flower; that Oscar Paterson has genius."

And the two friends, leaning over the manuscript on Wattman paper,[2] bound in willow-green silk, resumed reading in a loud voice, almost in chorus.

---

1 The interjections of dialogue by Maud and Lily are set in a different font in the *Écho de Paris* text of the story, but not in the *Journal* reprint, the example of which I have followed.

2 The intended reference is presumably to paper manufactured by the famous papermaker James Whatman, but I have left the spelling as it is rendered in the original; in French, a wattman was a tram-driver.

Princess Silviane is sad; she is thinking about the handsome princes clad in brocade, silver and white plumes, who brought their sisters from distant realms last spring. How many fanfares, silken standards and quivering banners there were! The streets hung with Flanders tapestries had never contained so many flag-bearers, armed cavaliers and trumpeters. And how many robust lads clad in tight buff leather there were in the escort of valentins around the beautiful brides!

Golden carriages ornamented with mirrors had brought the married couples at the trot of eight horses caparisoned in mauve silk, their foreheads bristling with plumes. Blismode and Gernière were queens today . . . and no one was marrying her because she was doubtless too young or not yet sufficiently formed, too delicate to please the handsome princely heirs avid for descendants! And the gentle Silviane remained solitary in the garden of orange trees and cypresses, trying to console herself, poor soul, with a golden ball.

"It's delightful," put in Miss Lily, "delightful! But here comes the tea and the toast; let's make room on the side-table for Betsy to put her tray down." And when Betsy, very comic-opera in her flowery calico dress with a bib pinned to her bodice and her pretty arms bare, had deposited the so-called peacock-feather Minturne faience teapot on the mahogany side-table, and Maud Beecocosme had got up to go and fetch the bottles of gin and whisky from the cupboard, all the esthetic soul of which was to wash down the tea, and they had both ingurgitated a modicum of twenty rounds of buttered toast with anchovies and caviar, Miss Lily struck a pose that was even more lilial, if possible, putting her elbow on the table and describing a curve as harmonious as a swan's neck with her arm, and the two friends, having bathed their gazes in one another's eyes, resumed in a languid voice, almost in chorus: "O my heart . . . !"

It was a decorated golden ball, but with a smooth surface, because it was the handiwork and the gift of a fay. Scarcely having been touched, it leapt of its own accord to the level of the tallest trees, to fall back gently on to the grass of a lawn, animated by a magical life. Silviane's godmother had recommended her never to neglect or lose that precious plaything; the enchanted ball would find her a husband, but she must never be separated from it, under the penalty of remaining unwed forever. And Princess Silviane, who was of a loving nature, slightly curious and desirous of the unknown, played with the ball every day.

"Oh," Miss Lily suddenly burst forth, "in truth, are you not shocked? Is not Oscar Paterfield[1] trying to indicate some impropriety there? Reply, my soul, in all sincerity. Personally, I don't like that solitary game of the amorous princess with the animate ball that rebounds continually."

Miss Lily's faded cornflower blue eyes were rolling and swerving now like those of an automaton; upon which Maud Beecocosme, while biting a slice of toast,

---

1 This variation in the fictitious author's name is present in both newspaper versions of the story. The choice of Paterson/Paterfield as a pseudonym for the Wildean writer associates him with Walter Pater, the principal critic of the English Esthetic Movement.

said, after a moment's reflection: "No, truly, I don't see it. If there were two balls instead of one, perhaps . . . yes, perhaps one could . . . But then again, Oscar Paterfield is an honest man, quite incapable of wanting to trouble the quietude of two well-brought-up young women, and since you're to take the role in his magical pantomime, be reassured, my desired dove, that you can juggle with all the balls he offers you in complete security, even if they're made of gutta-percha. But let's resume the story of the golden ball."

So, Princess Silviane was sitting, that evening, even sadder than all the other evenings, next to the marble basin furrowed by red fish. Nonchalantly leaning back on the pedestal of one of the faience lions, with the enchanted ball in her hand, she was thinking, the poor abandoned child, about the evenings of old when she and her sisters, as they were young girls, danced innocently, holding hands, under the orange trees and cypresses of the park; the golden oranges shone in the gleaming foliage and, molded in long transparent dresses, their chignons dotted with primroses, they strove to recall in their poses the dancing group of the immortal Fresco, for they were very esthetic princesses, well versed in the study of Carpaccios and Botticellis, of which they would have been able to furnish Burne-Jones with a few attitudes.

"Oh, what's that, my dear soul? Don't you find that Oscar Paterson is becoming humorous here? I ask you, why that attack on Burne-Jones, our national glory?"

"Oh, not as national as all that, since he consents to

paint portraits of little French comtesses; and then, my beloved ewe, it's no longer Burne-Jones that it's necessary to find mad, but Blake, Blake and Blake forever. But let's get back to the pantomime."

And she was so distracted, the poor little princess, that the golden ball slipped from her fingers and rolled into the water of the basin. It went down the twelve marble steps and then disappeared. There was consternation. No more ball, no more husband; the princess remained stupefied by it, putting her hands together, and then dissolved in tears. She wept for a long time, a very long time, and her despair was so great that the peacocks, folding up their tails, quit the park discreetly.

"Oh! Oh!" cried Beecocosme, "those peacocks are folding up their tails to indicate that the poor princess will no longer find a husband; it's symbolism of the finest and most delicate sort, isn't that true, Lily?"

"Yes, but all those tails folding up at once will make a lot of noise; that will distract the audience; no one will be paying any attention to my tears, and I know how to weep divinely, my dear. I followed the performances of Madame Bernhardt last season at the Gaité theater."

"But you know full well, dear delight, that the peacocks of the park are played by feather fans; they don't make any noise."

"Yes, you're right; let's continue the reading."

And the little princess would have wept indefinitely if a sticky and monstrous big-bellied frog had not surged forth from the depths of the water and, trailing its goiter, had not slowly and heavily climbed the twelve marble steps to come and crouch before the sad princess, with the golden ball in its paws.

"Oh, yes, that's the jolliest scene in the tale, when the Frog Prince, the enchanted frog, comes to propose to the king's daughter that he will return the enchanted ball to her on condition that she lets him sit beside her at the table, eat from her plate and lie with her in her bed for one night. I'm truly very anxious about that scene of the third act, when I have to take the frog to bed. Is this Joe Cold, who is to play the role of the Frog Prince, at least a decent fellow? Do you know him well, my lovely?"

To which Miss Beecocosme replied: "I know that he's studying at Oxford, and you know as well as I do what respect the students of Oxford have for ladies; he's a very reserved fellow, but very handsome and a particular friend of Oscar's."

"Of Oscar's, in truth? And very handsome, you say?"

To which Miss Beecocosme replied, without blinking: "I saw him bathing last summer at Brighton."

"At Brighton! Without swimming trunks, then?"

"Without swimming trunks. He's very handsome, I assure you, and will play the role perfectly."

"Oh, I'm sincerely enchanted—but give me a few details,"

Maud and Lily did not get any further with *The Frog Prince* that day

LITTLE TALES OF AUTUMN

(*L'Écho de Paris*, 23 October, 30 October, 14 November & 29 November 1894)

I

ABOUT forty years ago, in the old small villas of the bourgeoisie and the magistracy, one could encounter in certain old, proper and discreet petty bourgeois families, dear creatures treated less as hirelings than as friends, who did not always live under the same roof but who spent three or four days of the week there, relegated to the family linen-closet and scrupulously occupied with the household's work of sewing and mending.

Those needlewomen—chatterboxes, as the impertinent persiflage of the eighteenth-century, of which they seemed to be a part, dubbed them—were the joy of the entire provincial infancy, today ripened in their forties. They were old spinsters, somewhat devoted, somewhat finicky and somewhat gossipy, whom our parents would only have tolerated mockingly in the servants' parlor, but to whom children were confided in order to take them to their grandparents; and, grouped in the large hall encumbered with cupboards, the oldest of those sweet old ladies told captivating stories.

And with that, there were manias for six o'clock mass, which could not be missed for anything in the world, cooking-pots with embers dormant under their ashes that they transported in all weathers—rain, snow and squalls—shielding them under a corner of their cloak, the most formal obstinacy in not taking their place at a table where there was cutlery arranged in a cross, bizarre devotions and petty saints of faience that they always carried, buried in the depths of some immense pocket in their skirts, a priceless fashion of making the sign of the cross before every oath, and chinoiseries, and grimaces, and reverences!

I knew one of those poor and touching women, named Nanon, who came to my grandmother's house during the day, where she was charged with all the mending in the house. She had been pretty once and had had a well-intentioned gallant, but Nanon had never wanted to quit her old infirm parents. One morning the lover had wearied of waiting for Nanon, and Nanon was now growing old alone in her little seamstress's lodgings, with the memory of those old folk, who had died not long after, and perhaps the regret of the departed lover. Nanon was greatly liked in our house; she was an old spinster, with manias, but upright and honest; she never lied.

I sense a melancholy invading me, however, in wanting to evoke that frail and faded silhouette; all the ashes of the past have come to velvet with precocious snow these tales that I want to be joyful, and I have slipped in spite of myself into the indescribable attraction exhaled by that little autumnal town, that little fortified town bearing the stamp of the last century, with its belfry, its quincunxes and the tall houses with sculpted gables of its market-place. And under the slight and discreet footsteps of the poor faded shadow, I am afraid of seeing other shadows surge forth, which are dear to me; and there is a kind of bleak excursion of specters through the deserted streets, with cobblestones framed by grass, of my natal town.

Brrr! Brrr! Brrr . . . ! But in the end, as Nanon herself used to say, "with a pinch of tobacco and a cup of coffee one can mock the devil." Here, then, is the first of Nanon's tales, such as she told it in her own somewhat particular language, when my cousins and I were grouped around her knees in my grandmother's linen-closet.

Well, Mademoiselles prattlers and you, Monsieur sleeper-awake, know that there was once a rich, powerful and highly decorated seigneur marquis called Monsieur Du Tillet d'Ajurincourt. He had lived for a long time in Paris and also at Versailles, where he had done things that were not very nice, so it was said, for this happened under Louis XV, before that slut of a Revolution. Out there he had frequented people of all sorts, bankers and alchemists—in sum, a whole heap of specimens better suited to hold court with Hell than with the Church. It was said that he had participated in the *Great Work*. What that was, the people of the homeland would have had difficulty saying, but it was (at this point Nanon made the sign of the cross) the ultimate abomination.

So, when he returned to the homeland, in a bad way, no one in the nobility cared to see a man so compromised; he was said to be more dead than alive—but the little Vidame de Gondrecoeur, one morning, couldn't stand it any longer; he had known the old marquis, when he was a child, in his father's house; so he set off, eaten up with curiosity, for Du Tillet's domain.

It was mid-autumn; the plane-trees were already yellow and there were false twenty-franc coins on the lawns. He arrived at the entrance to the park, asked for the gate to be opened, leapt briskly from his berline and stopped dead, astonished to learn that Monsieur le Marquis, whom he had believed to be in bed spitting his soul at God, was in the process of making a tour of the park. He hurried on, and at the far end of the most royal avenue, what did he see? As straight as a rush, his expression arrogant, a cane with a golden pommel in his hand, the old Marquis d'Ajurincourt in person—who, as sprightly as a young man, seeing him at a distance, called out to him, and said, in a falsetto tone, his fist proudly planted on his hip:

"Well, Vidame, you've come to see whether I'm not dead? They're saying in town that I'm on my deathbed. You can see that I'm quite well—ha ha! I'm taking a turn around my park, and fresh air doesn't frighten me!" And he added, in a singularly sharp voice: "And no priest or physician in my house! What need have I of that breed? I'm bearing my sixty years rather well, admit it, young man!"

And, striking with an authoritarian thrust of his cane the ground encumbered with dead leaves: "I come here to make my tour of the park every evening; the sunsets here are splendid, admit it. I'm here this evening and I'll come many other evenings yet, and the money-lenders that it inconveniences will have nothing to say about it, ha ha ha!"

The Vidame de Gondrecourt reported afterwards that he had a strange impression of malaise then. The marquis had suddenly appeared to him so singularly thin in the crepuscular autumnal avenue that a slight cemetery chill ran down between his shoulders; that haughty and sarcastic silhouette, profiled in black against the crimson of the sky had reminded him then, forcefully, with his odd smile and his sunken and shining eyes, of that of a certain Monsieur Voltaire, a pagan of the same genre as Monsieur le Marquis, who was worth no better.

He took his leave rather precipitately, without the great rascal of a marquis taking the trouble to escort him, rapidly rejoined his berline and "*hup! whip, coachman, a good tip for the postillion,*" returned to the ramparts of the town at a gallop, where the first news that he learned on stopping at the gate was that the marquis had died the previous day.

But the vidame had just seen him, and talked to him, in that château visited by death, that château of dream and phantasmagoria where unreal valets, presumably shades, had received him!

"I come here to make my tour of the park every evening; the sunsets here are splendid, admit it. I'm here this evening and I'll come many other evenings yet."

The vidame had a bad fever because of it, which sent him incontinently to bed—"And," added good old

Nanon, with a fearful and contrite expression, "the worst thing is that the evil marquis kept his word; he still walks every evening in full court dress in his grand avenue of plane trees. He's twenty years old when one encounters him there again." And Nanon cited the names of people she had known. "Which proves," she concluded, in the manner of an evangelical moral, that the devil never dies and that evil still exists."

We did not understand very well, I confess, how the marquis, who was dead, could stroll in his park, converse there with the vidame, and return again even a hundred years later, but we were delightfully moved, and we shivered with all our palpitating little souls at Nanon's mysterious intonations and fearful interruptions; she was a marvelous story-teller, since she impassioned her audience; she believed what she recounted, that is the whole of it, and when she had finished mumbling her delusions at us, we said to her: "More, Nanon, more!"

It is necessary not to demand any more of a tale.

II

These were tales told for invalids, tales for the heavy atmospheres of chambers of tisanes and hot infusions, tales told between six and seven o'clock, the hour when fevers rise, which Nanon was invited to come and recite in a dreamlike voice at our bedside, that of a child excessively loved.

She entered on tiptoe the room already woven in shadow, slipping in quietly, installed herself at the head of our little bed, and commenced in her blank voice.

＊

Three white cats cravated with ribbons are dancing around a cauldron. They drink good milk therefrom and one of them dips a claw into it hesitantly, the greedy little thing, and leaps backwards in three bounds, mewling. Three white cats cravated in ribbons are dancing round a cauldron.

The old crow perched in the corner of the window considers them carefully with half-closed eyes. One cannot tell whether he is asleep or awake, the old crow with ragged plumage, almost a hundred years old, perched in the corner of the window in the shadow of the curtains.

Perhaps he is thinking about the great gleaming woods of cypress and pines, where he flew at full tilt in its youth, deafening the surrounding country with his sisters, Mesdames the Rooks: *couac, couac, couac!*

Perhaps the old crow is also thinking about fresher April skies, when, through the forests in bud, the nests accumulated, built amid chatter, and there was joy, abundance and amour. Oh, why did that accursed woodcutter break his wing? A stone thrown with a fine malice! And a sea of rancor swells the heat of the old bird.

On the window-sill, there is a little Saxe statuette, an ancient little shepherdess with pink make-up, who has been miming the same curtsey for two hundred years. Oh, my God, how bored she must be! There is also a Christ in blue Quimper faience and a sand-glass that is never turned over.

All these objects are velveted with dust; the Christ is the color of ash and the little old Saxe, shrouded with spider-webs, is desperate, so desperate that she is shaking her crook and furbelows vainly in an immobile gesture. As for the sand-glass, it is asleep; in any case, it has been in the room for so long that the other objects no longer even seem to know that it is there. The old calendar hanging next to the mantelpiece in at least twenty-five years old; ancient engravings, which might be Holbeins, are fading of their own accord behind their unpolished glass; the antique pendulum clock in its waxed walnut case is more reminiscent of a sarcophagus; there is no tick-tock or patter of the feet of mice in the dusty abandonment of the old dwelling.

The three white cats cravated with ribbon are dancing around the cauldron and the crow is devouring and ruminating his bile. Oh, when the old fay Carabosse,[1] who resides in this lair, comes back from her walk on the ramparts, he will regain his courage and his energy one last time, it seems to me. He will fly into her face and, stunning her with the thrusts of his large beak, will wait until the old crone is completely unconscious in order to peck out her eyes at his leisure. Oh, to dig into them with his long beak and empty her old eye-sockets slowly . . . And the old crow fluffs up his feathers; *couac!* He flaps his wings, and a ferocious joy dilates and fills them: *couac, couac, couac!* It is not with impunity that one has had a few ancestors at Montfaucon; the noblesse of the gibbet obliges!

1 The fay Carabosse was invented by Madame d'Aulnoy in one of her *contes de fées*, and became the archetype of the "bad fay" who curses children in the cradle instead of blessing them, as required by custom. The name became generic.

But, click and squeak, a key turns in the lock; someone has come into the space behind the bed, and Madame Gorgibus, wrapped in her mantle of puce silk, pleated and hooded, comes into the old abode, She brings to her old crow—oh, how far she is from suspecting the blackness of his soul!—a piece of soft veal, the odor of which disarms the sly beast, and then she runs to the fireplace and crouches down in the ashes with all her cats climbing up her. "Get off! Stop, Blanchette, you'll be beaten! Do you want a slap, Frimousse?" She sips the milk, find it just right, closes the interior shutter of the little casement, puts Messire Crow in his wicker cage, with a piece of calico on top, the shade of which will send him to sleep, lights her old lamp with a green shade, pulls an old armchair with earpieces next to the hearth and settles down for a nap before the evening supper. The three white cats, stretching in the gentle warmth, are purring in her lap.

Master Crow, captive, is asleep in his dark cage in a corner of the room. Once again, poor Madame Gorgibus will not be murdered tonight!

III[1]

Princess Mandosiane was six hundred years old; For six centuries she lived, embroidered in velvet with a face and hands of painted silk. She was entirely clad in pearls, with a necklace so heavy with embroidery that it bulged, and

---

1 Lorrain reprinted this section of the portmanteau separately in *Princesses d'ivoire et d'ivresse* as "Mandiosane captive" (tr. in *Masks in the Tapestry*). The other sections of the story were also reprinted, with individual titles attached, in various collections.

the arabesques of her robe, woven in silver fabric, were the most delicate golden thread.

An ultramarine mantle patterned with anemones was fastened over her breast by veritable precious stones, and sapphire cabochons ornamented the hem of her dress.

She had figured for a long time in processions and royal fêtes. She was brought out then, hoisted on a flagpole, and the glitter of her jewels delighted queens and common folk. They were happy times, when, through the paved streets, beneath the flutter of flamboyant pennants, Princess Mandosiane was acclaimed. Then she was returned ceremoniously to the treasure of the cathedral and she was shown to foreigners in exchange for copious gold.

There was no marvel like that miraculous princess. She was born of the dream and the obstinate toil of twenty nuns, who, for fifty years, had labored extracting the delightful and hieratic figure from skeins of silk and silver.

Her hair was yellow silk; two tourmalines of the most beautiful blue had been incrusted at the location of her irises, and she was holding a sheaf of white velvet lilies, placed over her heart.

Then the era of processions passed; thrones were abolished; kings disappeared; civilization made progress; and the princess of pearls and painted silk remained confined henceforth to the shadow of the cathedral.

She spent her days there in the half-light of a crypt, with a heap of bizarre things grimacing in the corners. There were ancient statues, tankards beside ciboria, old church ornaments, copes still stiff, as if gilded by the sun, slowly fading away in the night, with the chalices that were no longer used by officiants. There was also an old Christ backed up in a corner, completely veiled in spiders' webs.

The door of the subterranean chapel was never opened. All those old things lay dormant there, buried and forgotten. And a great despair gripped the heart of Princess Mandosiane.

She lent her ear to the counsel of a red mouse, an insidious little mouse, as quick as lightning, tenacious and willful, which had already been pestering her for years.

"Why are you obstinate in remaining a captive, trussed up in all the pearls and embroideries that wrap you? It's no life, yours. You've never lived, even in the times when you were resplendent beneath the blue sky of carilloned fêtes, acclaimed by the intoxication of crowds, and now, you see, it's oblivion and death. If you wanted, with my sharp teeth, I'd loosen one by one the silken stitches and the golden cord that have held you in place, motionless, for six hundred years, in that shiny velvet—which, between us—no longer has much of a gleam.

"It might perhaps cause you a little pain, especially when I pick out stitches close to the heart, but I'd begin with the long contours, those of the hands and the face, and you'd already be able to stretch and move, and you'd see how good it is to breathe and live! Beautiful as you are, with your face of a folktale princess, and rich with the fabulous treasure with which your garment is respondent, you'd be dressed by the greatest designers; you'd be taken for the daughter of a banker, and marry, at the very least, a French prince.

"You have millions in pearls on you! Come on, let me set you free; you'll revolutionize the world.

"If you only knew how good it is to be free, to breathe in the wind, filling your lungs, and follow your own whim! You're decked out in those opals and sapphires like a knight in armor, and you've never even fought in battle. I know the roads that lead to the land of Wellbeing. Let yourself blossom outside your embroidered sheath; we'll go around the world together and I promise you a throne and the love of a hero."

Princess Mandosiane consented. The little red mouse immediately commenced its murderous work; his teeth sawed, cut and filed away the velvet eaten by mites; pearls tinkled as they fell, one by one, and on moonlit nights as in beautiful sunlit skies, in the crypt illuminated by a ventilation shaft, the red mouse cut and ate, always busy.

When it attacked the famous necklace of nacre and pearls, Princess Mandosiane had the sensation of a sharp cold in her heart.

For several days already she had felt shivery and lighter, and, singularly supple in the midst of all those broken stitches, she undulated in the fabric as if animated by a breeze, and waited, delightedly, for the mouse to finish its work.

When the rodent's teeth sank into her bosom, the poor princess of spangles and silk, this time, collapsed entirely. There was a something like a stream of ashes on the flagstones of the obscure chapel, the soft fall of fleecy silks, dismantled braid and luminous rags; a few cabochons rolled away like grains of wheat, and the old mite-ridden velvet of the banner tore from top to bottom.

Thus died Princess Mandosiane, for having listened to the insidious advice of a little mouse.

IV

Madame de Lautréamont lived in the most beautiful house in the city; it was the former residence of the general receiver of taxes, built under Louis XV—modestly!—its high ornamental windows evoked the admiration of everyone who passed through the main square on market days. There was a large main body flanked with two wings, linked by a set of railings; the main courtyard and the most beautiful garden in the world were, behind the central building; it descended in a series of terraces all the way to the edge of the ramparts, overlooking thirty leagues of countryside, and, with the finest Louis XV orderliness, sheltered in its boscage licentious statues, all more-or-less teased by Laughters and Amours.

As for the apartments, they were lined with sculpted wooden panels of the most charming effect, ornamented with pier-glasses, and the parquets of the entire ground floor, curiously encrusted with tropical hardwoods, gleamed like mirrors. Madame de Lautréamont lived in the main building; she had rented the detached part of the wings to reliable tenants and received a good income from them. There was no one who did not envy the inhabitants of the Hôtel Lautréamont and it was the sempiternal subject of conversations in the city.

Madame de Lautréamont was born with full hands and had always had all the luck: a husband built like Hercules, entirely devoted to her will, who let her dress herself in Paris from a great couturier; two children that she had established well, the daughter married to a king's prosecutor and the son already a captain of artillery or on the way to being one; the most beautiful house in the département; health that maintained her every youthful and authentically desirable at over forty-five years of age; and, to maintain that princely dwelling and that almost indecent health, a domestic such as one no longer sees, a phoenix, a rare pearl of a maidservant, all devotion, all attention and honesty incarnate: the worthy Gudule.

Thanks to that marvelous young woman Madame de Lautréamont contrived, with three domestics—a gardener, a valet de chambre and a cook—to maintain her immense house on an income of sixty thousand livres. It was without doubt the best-kept house in the city: not a speck of dust on the marble of the tables, parquets that were dangerous by dint of being waxed, old mirrors brighter than spring water, and everywhere, in all the apartments, an order and symmetry that led to the former tax-receiver's house being cited as the foremost in the province, with a phrase henceforth consecrated to designate a well-cared-for abode: "One might believe one were in the Lautréamont house."

The soul of that astonishing dwelling was found to be a worthy old spinster, with cheeks still fresh and naïve little blue eyes, who had a duster or a broom in her hand from morning till evening, serious, silent and active, who never stopped rubbing, brushing, dusting and making things shine: a declared enemy of every atom of dust. The other domestics were a little afraid of her; the worthy Gudule maintained a terrible surveillance. Entirely devoted to the service of her masters, nothing escaped her little blue eyes; she was always in the house as well, for the old woman only went out to attend mass on Sundays and feast days—not very devoted, in truth, and not assiduous at six o'clock mass, the old maidservants' pretext for going out every day.

In the city, people never tired of eulogizing that model of housekeepers, and Madame de Lautréamont's domestic was much envied. A few indelicate souls were even unscrupulous enough to try to steal her. Golden bridges were offered to Gudule, for vanity was mingled with it, and even in the society of Paris attempts were made to lure the poor woman from her mistress—but it was a waste of effort; Gudule, with a fidelity of another era, turned a deaf ear to all propositions, and Madame de Lautréamont's insolent good fortune continued until the day when the old maidservant, worn out and exhausted by labor, was extinguished, like a lamp devoid of oil, in her cold little attic under the eaves—where Madame de Lautréamont, it is necessary to say in her praise, stayed with her for three days.

The worthy Gudule had the joy of dying with her dear mistress by her bedside. The Lautréamonts gave their servant an appropriate funeral; Monsieur de Lautréamont led the mourners. Gudule had her concession in the cemetery, fresh flowers on her grave for at least a week—and then it was necessary to replace her.

Replace her? No, for that was impossible, but at least to introduce into the house a woman holding her employment. Housekeepers can be found, and after a few unsuccessful attempts, Madame de Lautréamont finally thought she could congratulate herself for having put her hand on a trustworthy young woman of the utmost probity; Madame Agathe reigned henceforth in the former house of the tax-collector. She was a rather strongly-built person, her bodice a bastion, who busied herself, gesticulating and alarming, in every corner, a bunch of keys in her belt and a changing silk apron around her waist, reminiscent of Madame Rodomont.[1] Her service was not exactly silent; there was nothing from morning till evening but screeching at the other domestics, and the old dwelling, so calm and so quiet in Gudule's time, was deafened by it. But Mademoiselle Agathe knew how to exert herself, and that is everything; there was nothing but daily reports on the antechamber and the servants parlor, and interesting discussions with the cook, and Madame de Lautréamont ended up by letting herself be captured by all those noisy manifestations of devotion.

Oh, it was no longer the service of Gudule, that invisible and silent service that one might think carried out by a shadow, those delicate and seemingly fearful attentions of a hidden devotion, that perpetual and minute vigilance of the old lady in adoration of her masters' house, that cult of devotion for her parish, and all the domestic fervor that had once put something like the

1 A rodomont is a braggart, named after Rodomonte, a character in the Italian mock-epic *Orlando inamorato*, who became a stock character in comedies staged by the Parisian Théâtre des Italiens.

126

perfume of an altar into the Lautréamonts' home. There were now specks of dust on the marble table-tops; the old glassware in the drawing rooms no longer replicated the transparent water of springs, nor did the parquets shine like mirrors; but habitude is such a force, and Gudule had created such a legend that the former house of the general tax-collector was still cited in current reflections as the best-kept house in the département.

One night, six months later—it was mid-November, Gudule having died in March—Madame de Lautréamont woke Monsieur de Lautréamont up abruptly and, in a slightly altered voice, without even lighting the candle, said to him: "That's singular, Hector. Listen! One might think it the sweep of Gudule's broom."

Monsieur de Lautréamont, in the very bad mood of a man half-asleep, snorted that she was mad; but a great emotion gripped Madame de Lautréamont and shook her with such a tremor that that model husband consented to wake up and lend an ear to his wife's divagations.

"I assure you that someone is there," she went on, "on the first floor landing. I can hear footsteps, but why that sound of a broom? Hold on, it's drawing away now, someone is sweeping the depths of the vestibule, and I assure you that it's her fashion of sweeping. You can suppose that I know it."

Madame de Lautréamont did not even dare pronounce the name of the old maidservant, and Monsieur de Lautréamont understood that.

"In truth, you have that old girl on the brain. You're dreaming while awake, my dear; I can assure you that there's nothing there. The air is so calm that one can't even hear a leaf stir. It's your dinner that isn't passing. Would you like me to make you a cup of tea?"

As if moved by a spring, however, Madame de Lautréamont, shivering all over, had leapt out of bed and, running barefoot across the room, opened the door slightly, and then closed it again with a terrible cry.

With one bound, Monsieur de Lautréamont was beside her, not understanding anything of that fit of madness, and he brought her back, almost inanimate, to a large armchair, into which she let herself fall, and suffocated for some time without being able to speak.

She finally found her voice, and, the bedroom, now being illuminated, she said: "It's her. I saw her as I see you; she was there, sweeping and polishing the parquet in the vestibule, in the coarse dress that is familiar to you, in a bonnet, as when she was alive, but so pale and so silent! Oh, what a face of the cemetery! It's necessary to have masses said for her, my friend!"

Monsieur de Lautréamont calmed his wife as best he could, but he remained anxious and pensive nevertheless; even more mysterious things have been seen.

The following night, Madame de Lautréamont's hallucination gripped her again. Shivering, her teeth clenched in terror, this time she heard the dead maidservant waxing and polishing the deserted landing, busy on her slippered feet. Was the fear contagious? In the silence of the great sleeping house, Monsieur de Lautréamont heard the noise this time, and in spite of his wife, who was clinging fearfully to his arm, he went boldly to open the door and looked out.

128

All the hairs stood on end in his moist flesh; the dismantled silhouette of the maidservant was agitating and dancing about, like a funereal marionette, in the middle of the deserted vestibule; the window that illuminated the stairway was bathing her in moonlight, and in the luminous blue radiance the dead woman was passing back and forth, brushing and rubbing, prey to a feverish agitation; one might have thought it the work of a damned soul, and as she passed before him, Monsieur de Lautreamont distinctly saw drops of sweat on her already-polished skull. He closed the door again abruptly, terrified and convinced.

"You're right," he said, simply, returning to his wife, "it's necessary to have a few masses said for that old girl."

Ten masses were said for the dead woman, ten low masses, which Monsieur and Madame de Lautrámont attended, and the worthy Gudule did not return again to do Mademoiselle Agathe's work on the clear nights of November.

V

And when I have recounted the apparition of Queen Maritorne, which weighed upon my entire childhood, I will have concluded the series of my little autumnal tales, and terminated the sequence of these faded stories with an old and obsolete perfume, with which Nanon enchanted my early years and which, at the present moment, still evoke in my eyes an entire corner of a province that has disappeared today, a society entirely forgotten, with the indefinable charm that certain hornbeam hedges and avenues of lindens exhale at the end of October: an insipid and piquant odor of cemetery soil, the perfume of ether and dead leaves.

Queen Maritorne[1] was the terror of greedy children and thieves; she reigned over the grain-loft, where pears and apples ripened, lined up in good order, until they went into the vat from which the wine was drawn; she was also the punishment of drunkards, and surged forth unexpectedly from barrels fraudulently pierced by an indelicate valet. No one had ever seen her, but she was known to be present and on watch everywhere; she was in the jam pot slyly caressed by the eyes of children, as in the shadows of the cupboards in the servants' parlor; the pot-bellied chest of drawers where the old folk packed away their boxes of marzipan and their jars full of humbugs and candied fruit, were also defended by her, and whoever risked opening the drawer of sweetmeats could very well find Queen Maritorne lying inside.

She had all rights over the gluttonous child who had made himself ill at table, and carried terrible indigestions in the pleats of her dress; she distributed fevers and colics like manna to the culpable, and every stomach in revolt was hers. She also resided in kitchens, lying in ambush behind jars of preserves and the enormous copper pans

1 In polite terms, a maritorne is a maidservant of the lowest status, but the word is more often used pejoratively as an approximate equivalent of the English "slattern."

in which civets of venison simmered in autumn; she also haunted obscure pantries and fruit-racks embalmed with the odor of medlars, and she obstructed large heaps of vegetables with shade.

Indistinct and vague as she was in the individual imagination, her obese and rotund silhouette weighed like a malaise over the conscience and stomach of infidel maidservants and naughty children. So, great was the terror of little Wilhem when, carried away from the table for having guzzled a plum tart and cream like a glutton, he was laid down in his bed, in his room, with the commencement of a stomach-ache, alone in the large room where he slept with his nursemaid, all alone in the third storey of that vast four-story house, while everyone else was still downstairs at dinner.

His nursemaid, in a hurry to rejoin the other domestics, had left him without a light, and through the high window, the curtains of which she had neglected to close, the bright moonlight entered, deploying an immense white sheet on the floor and congealing the indecisive contours of objects in bizarre attitudes.

And suddenly, in the haunted chamber, unknown profiles grimaced; firstly, under the glass of his frame, there was the faded pastel of the grandfather. With a high muslin cravat, a light brown jacket open over a ruffed shirt, he had the face of an ancient magistrate, as rigid as a monstrance. His eyebrows suddenly frowned and a flash of legitimate indignation lit up his eyes; colic twisted the unfortunate little Wilhem more forcefully, who swiftly turned his terrified eyes away. His gaze fell upon an armchair in which an equivocal pile of clothes lay in the shadow; slowly, the flaccid legs of trousers became animated, two unexpected feet emerging therefrom, while a torso loomed up in a sudden flutter of the jacket; two little muscular arms clutched a meager breast, and the head of a sinister old man sniggered in the silence. What a rictus! The thirty-two keys of the harpsichord appeared, all white, in the nut-cracker face of the bizarre little being.

But it was only an apparition. The room had fallen back into darkness, and when Wilhem, who had hidden his head under the sheets, hazarded a frightened eye out of the covers, nothing abnormal could any longer be seen; everything had resumed its accustomed place; it was as if the objects drowned in the half-light had faded into the night, and hardly anything remained but an anxiety on the subject of his water-jug, placed on the chest of drawers and eccentrically crouched in the middle of its bowl like an enormous white toad.

Little Wilhem commenced to respire—but his quietude did not last long. An unusual noise soon made him prick up his ears. Someone was coming upstairs now, and there were footsteps, footsteps and more footsteps, like the tramp of an army on the march. A mob was hastening up the stairs, and he heard jostling on the landing of the floor below, spreading up toward his own, surely coming to his room.

And in a great flood of light his door opened brutally. He could not even utter a scream. The entire battery of kitchen utensils was there, lurching over the threshold; there were scintillating copper saucepans full to the brim with rice and bread soup, immense bowls of preserves were waddling heavily on three unequal feet, and Savoy biscuit-mills, and kettles with maleficent expressions, and ill-intentioned teapots with metallic reflections, and coffee-pots with long insidious spouts and hostile attitudes. All of them were bustling, bumping into one another and penetrating in silence into the middle of the room; it was like a swarm of phantasmal objects crawling over the floor; they surrounded the bed, and climbed slowly up the bedclothes, like a mute tide, only to fall back and climb again.

Bathed in sweat, his eyes widened by fear, the child could not pronounce a word; it was an utterly terrifying invasion; the room was full of all those dream pots and pans, which he could still see coming through the door, and, mingling with the surly kettles and menacing coffee-pots there were now sausages with feet, hams with the faces of gnomes, and phantom chickens fluttering around the room, all skewered and ready-roasted.

The heads of jugged hares lifted up the lids of saucepans; the chirping beaks of larks were trying to escape from another, purées of beans and large peas were sizzling and bursting bubbles in earthenware pots; a goose basted with lard was dancing a can-can; a stuffed fowl ready for the spit and pigeons escaped from the stove were forming a cortege of boiled flesh for a fricasseed rabbit. It was something frightful, and in that fantastic culinary apparatus Wilhem recognized Queen Maritorne.

She was there, giant and impassive, fully armored in red copper, advancing slowly in her heavy bell-shaped robe, her waist imprisoned by a soup tureen. What could be seen of her skin was rissoled and gilded like the stomach of a roasted turkey that had cooked for a long time over the kitchen fire, and she had two enormous hen's feet for hands. She was a horrible creature, bald and hairless, with the tail of a peacock, ornamented and dressed for the table, deployed on her head. A necklace of saveloys dangled over the faience of her breast and two monstrous chitterlings hung down to her waist in the manner of fancy ear-rings. In one hand she was holding a bouquet of leeks, onions and carrots, and she was brandishing an immense ladle in the other, a true queen of the cooking-pot, drawing purées, roux, sauces and broths relentlessly therefrom, and she menaced the terrified child with them.

But what he could not bear was the eye of that spectral doll: an automatic eye, enameled and lifeless, which was staring at him. He contrived a loud scream . . . and woke up this time to the light of a lamp and a candle; his mother, his sisters and his nursemaid hastened around him.

He woke up crestfallen, with a discomfited expression—little Wilhem had wet the bed.

PRINCESSES OF DARKNESS
(*Le Journal*, 19 & 23 April 1896)

"THE kiss of Satan rendered her beautiful. One Sunday, the church closed before her, and, pushed by the menace of brutal hands, she fled into the heath, everywhere that rebellious and wild nature created the hope of liberty."

Princesses of darkness . . . Jules Bois or Michelet said somewhere that the long amorous soliloquy of woman with herself created the devil. The devil is woman's own desire having taken form, her alerted sensuality awakening her and charming her; the evil influence of the beyond is her own troubled and mysterious soul offered to her soul in a mirror, and the princess of darkness springs forth spontaneously, like an accursed flower, into a realm created by her: hysteria—that frightening paroxysm of instincts and sexuality, a disconcerting deformation of femininity itself, in which the obsessed victim struggles, simultaneously sovereign and victim of the most delirious and baleful visions.

Princesses of darkness . . . for the occultism of which this atheistic *fin-de-siècle* has an unhealthy curiosity, has seen a blossoming for four years, in literature at least, of several venomous heroines. The novels of the young school are all haunted, today, by the dolorous profiles of women in ecstasy, more or less transported, lips agape and staring eyes fixed on a perilous beyond. The somewhat nebulous mysticism of the Romantics has been succeeded by crepuscular prose works in which the cult of Satan radiates a wild and troubling glare; to the inspired visages of saints we prefer the bewildered mask of suffering of witches. With Baudelaire, whose *Litanies de Satan* we all know by heart, we have listened to the promising and deceptive voice of despair; the women marked by his irreparable kiss are, of them all, those who attract us the most; they pass through the equivocal splendor of maleficent landscapes at the evil hour of dusk; Félicien Rops is their painter, Joris-Karl Huysmans their historian, Paul Adam their poet, and Jules Bois their shepherd.

They are the flock of damned women; their description is ever the same. Like Madame Chantelouve in *Là-Bas* and Paul Adam's Mahaut in his fine novel *Être*[1] they all have immeasurably widened eyes in excessively pale faces, the color of camphor or nacre, flesh resembling a host, and in their long bloodless necks, in their silhouettes of seeresses, either too curvaceous or too straight, they have the suppleness of reptiles rearing up and crawling by turns. Something akin to invisible hands pushes them forward in the shadows, and in the swish of their eternal black dresses they draw, God knows where, males breathless with desire and mute with dread. Woe

---

1 *Là-Bas* was first published in 1891, *Être* in 1888.

betide anyone who puts his hand in their petite hot or icy hand, for the princess of darkness is always ablaze or frozen; the hysteria that devours her makes her as ardent as hot coals or freezes the blood in her veins, and in the Middle Ages, the old charters assert, that frigidity of the flesh alternating with the heat of the blood was one of the key characteristics of demonism, and it required no more, as late as the year 1500, to tie a woman to the stake of a pyre.

That voluptuous body, supple, curvaceous and cold, in which the lust of Durtal, exasperated and sharpened, suddenly ignites abrupt ardors, Madame Chantelouve possessed. Like all demoniacs, the hysterical creature has the gift of provoking all embraces by undressing. When he drinks her kiss, Durtal thinks he is eating snow, while her hard breasts, throbbing against his breast, set fire to his marrow and his loins; during orgasm she has strange steely eyes, in which fumes rise, and from refusal to refusal, from rendezvous to rendezvous, where does that woman who has known the love of a priest and all the shame of adultery finally conduct her lover? To the Black Mass, where that galvanized cadaver suddenly abandons herself, in a room in a hovel, in order to initiate the wretch in the caresses of prisoners.

The princess of the princesses of darkness, Monsieur Huysmans has created there.

In Paul Adam's *Mystère des foules*[1]—for I will not insist on the heroine of *Être*, a study of Medieval sorcery—Annie, the poor and virginal niece of the Bishop

---

1 *Mystère des foules* was first published in 1895.

of Nancy, is nevertheless a tenebrous and demonic creature. Molded in the eternal black dress, which is the livery of them all, the svelte and pale heroine has the nacreous face, the large pure eyes and the gliding gait of her sisters. As chaste as the Virgin of evil, she only abandon her lips and fingers to men as far as is necessary to ignite their covetousness; the mystery of her body she keeps for Satan, her master, and, raised in the cathedral in the midst of ciboria and altar-cloths, that stained-glass saint—in appearance, at least—she does not lead men to the Black Mass, but to nocturnal assemblies in which the destiny of peoples is debated, to the modern sabbat of political meetings in which parliamentary infamies and fratricidal killings are decided. That little sister of the poor with an evangelical silhouette coldly elaborates the crushing of the proletariat to the profit of capital, of gold.

She is the princess of political darkness, the fervent adherent of evil for evil's sake.

Alongside those two figurines of shadow patiently sculpted and chiseled by two master artists, each incarnating a type so contrasted, although both molded in darkness and sulfur, one might believe that there is no place for a third entity of the Gulf. All the demoniacs who have filed past for eight years and are still filing past, whether sprouted from the seed-bed of Bodin[1] or in novels in the contemporary taste, are inevitably sisters

---

1 Jean Bodin (c1530-1596) was one of the most famous French writers on demonology; his *De la démonomanie des sorciers* (1580) became a standard witch-hunting manual during the panic of the seventeenth century.

of those two, and one could truly have made the same reproach to Satanism as to Virtue, the darkness being quite monotonous, when, among all those accursed flowers, a species of mandrake surged forth with a ragged and bloody flower that can, by right, take its place, if not the first, at least the third, in that flora of evil, for it displays its nature proudly in its title: *La Princesse des Ténèbres* by Monsieur Jean de Childra.[1]

La Princesse des ténèbres—a petty Parisienne exiled to a province in de Childra's novel—declares herself thus in a conversation with the fiancé that she does not love. Hysterical, demoniac or hallucinated, Madeleine Deslande,[2] a somewhat unhealthy daughter of a librarian, is suffering, above all, from embarrassment at the mediocrity of her milieu. The author does not say so explicitly, but in deceptively skillful scenes he puts in front of the reader a young woman tormented by vague dreams of a strange and curious traveler.

"He had beneath the white fog a livid face, in which one remarked above all the bloody beardless lips. His did not move, looking at her in an outrageous fashion,

1 Lorrain renders this pseudonym as it might have been intended to be rendered by its author, who usually signed herself Rachilde— although Alfred Jarry recorded that it was supposed to be "de Chilra", thus constituting a "perfect anagram"—but the printer of the actual first edition of the book (published in 1895) did not, rendering it as "de Chibra." The misprint in question created enduring confusion for later bibliographers.

2 As to whether Jean Lorrain ever took Rachilde to the salon of the flamboyant socialite Madeleine Deslandes, who—as previously noted—signed her own literary works "Ossit," we can only speculate, but the coincidence of names is intriguing.

planted straight and tall in the fluidifying fog, like a tree, a spontaneous florescence of mysterious shadows . . . and Madeleine discovered a dog behind him: a scarcely reassuring dog, very thin, high on its paws with a square muzzle and pointed ears; a shiny black animal with short hair that seemed moist."

That nocturnal peasant has stopped in Madeleine's garden, before the open window where she is belatedly doing needlework. Jean de Childra has planted in a few lines, and instantly, one shivers in divining that it is *Him*: the great lord and prince of darkness, whose intermittent presence next to the possessed individual will become the enigma and the impassioning figure of the book.

And already the demoniac, the marked and predestined woman, the petty bourgeoise, is acquiring indelible stigmata; her blonde hair becomes coppery, with strange reflections, and her pallor intensifies. Like the elect of Satan she has a disgust and ennui for real life, for housework and everything that surrounds her, and when, in the little drawing room where her senile relatives are busy around a spirit-tilted side-table "she surged forth fearfully, straight in her rigid black cashmere dress, like a sword suddenly drawn under a mourning drape, her fists clenched, her eyes fulgurant and her hair with ardent glints similar to flames, crying with a voice that was no longer her own: 'Do not evoke the dead here; I forbid it,'" the apparition is already no longer of this world; the young woman, who howls like a wounded bitch afraid of death, has already sensed him in the shadows, and that is the desperate cry of a witch fearful of becoming one.

A witch! She is one already, M. de Childra's little

Madeleine Deslande, when she escapes from the paternal house to run recklessly through the fields to reach the mountain—an old mountain all rocks and sands—where she loves to lie for hours on a flat stone, her hair undone and her eyes staring at the clouds. The Elect of Satan all have the grim love of solitude, and at all times the witch has fled toward the heaths where rebel and savage nature offers the hope of liberty.

"She leaned on the rocks and watched the sky, bluer and starrier, nothing but a hermetic vault of russet clouds. She undid her hair, enabling it to float in the fiery air, and she imagined that the torsades, in scattering, were spreading madly from one horizon to the other. A bitter smile creased her lips; Madeleine rediscovered herself there in her own realm, and reigned there with the birds of prey. Intoxicated by her beloved solitude, however, she always waited there for something, if not for someone. It was there that she had seen, or thought she had seen, one afternoon in August . . . my God, would she never finish doubting? She tipped back her head, her eyes ablaze with radiation closed . . ."

And the man reappears, the thin man, so svelte that one might have thought him a prodigious plant bearing a human head, the man in a dark costume, neither gray nor black, shining like the pelt of his dog, devoid of pleats or seams, with the monstrous watchful beast at his feet, flattened in a grim passion for his unknown master.

And as the hallucinated young woman, more fasci-nated still, hesitates fearfully before the man with the silhouette of a plant and the somber dog that never barks: "His name is Silence, for he is deaf," the stranger

replies to Madeleine's fear, "and my name is Hunter."
Hunter: doubtless the hunter and predator of souls, the bird-catcher of all wills and all resistances—and the scene of temptation is adorable.

"You have wanted it, Madeleine; I am finally emerging victorious from the rotten entrails of death. Summoned by you from afar, your adorable charity has extracted me once again from the void. You love me, I AM! Oh, my pale sister of folly, I shall, therefore, have drawn the sacred aliment from the golden harvest of your hair. I shall have drunk all my eternity in the clear springs of your eyes! Henceforth, you see, my desires will cling exclusively to your white neck, as furious birds strike their cage with their beaks! Understand well! The line of your white neck will be the limit . . . the limit . . . Madeleine, the hour has sounded of realizations of the impossible! You and me! The rest of the world no longer exists, and one day . . . one day I shall carry away your head, far away, in my two hands, like a chalice! Your predestined brain will have flowed into me, and not for any reason will its intoxicating liquor escape; I shall put on your mute lips the seal of purity that is called the bitterness of tears! You shall weep, and you shall cause weeping . . . for infinite despair springs forth from the great, the only sensuality, Madeleine!"

And, taking in both hands the poor head with dilated pupils, only sustaining it by its delicate neck, already trying almost to decapitate her, the stranger intoxicates Madeline with his kisses and the immeasurable pride of his singing phrases.

"Hunter," she murmurs, dully, "take my soul. I am yours."

It is the eternal scene of emprise; Madeleine has created herself the specter that bewitches her: "You love me, therefore I am." The sinister Hunter, the accursed silhouette, of which the hysterical virgin will die, is the work of her pride and her ennui. "You have wanted it, Madeleine, I am finally emerging victorious from the rotten entrails of death." The demoniac bears within herself the demon that obsesses her; the long amorous soliloquy of woman has created the Devil.

※

The Pact

You shall weep and you shall cause weeping.

"God does not exist. The only god is the one I love. The universe is a dream of which he is the creator. The laws of humanity are abolished because he has wished it. I curse my birth and I aspire to death, because he will unite himself with me beyond the here of this world. Virgin or woman, I swear to serve him for my happiness and my despair. If, by chance, my parents tread one day on a corner of his mantle, I will kill my parents, and if he is thirsty I shall express the pure water of the eyes of my new-born to enable him to drink."

That Credo of Evil, which is, in sum, nothing but the Catholic act of faith in reverse—since, in order to gain paradise, the church says to the faithful: "You will quit your father and mother and all those you love in order to follow the Lord"—studies of Satanism have made, approximately, the pact of the Prince of Darkness with his future princess. For the ensorcelled woman to become a witch in her turn, however, the indicated formula is perhaps unnecessary, since the demon evoked by the woman is, in sum, only a form of her desire. Sprung from her pride and slowly brooded in her hours of ennui, that fiancé of shadow appears to the spouse as if kneaded from her dreams, bloody with all her suffering, swollen with all her rancor, as changing and multiform as hysteria itself.

Woman? Throughout all times the demon has been her solitary sin, for she is, like the sea and the moon, those two cosmic femininities, always dreaming. It is for the eternal Eve, the woman thrice over, predestined to all the errors of the senses and the imagination, that Baudelaire wrote the melancholy wishes of the *Bienfaits de la Lune*:

"You shall love what I love and what loves me: water, the clouds, silence, the night, the immense green sea, formless and multiform water, the place where you will not be, the lover that you will not know, monstrous flowers, the perfumes that trouble the will, the cats that swoon on pianos and moan like women, in a hoarse and soft voice."

The lover that you will not know, the place where you will not be: all demonianism is in those two sad prophesies; the witch is insatiably amorous of the unknown, under the double influence of death and the night; her puberty, which awakens in her, causes her to quiver on the threshold of mystery; grim toward man, whom she fears in desiring him, curious with regard to phantoms,

144

avid for chimeras, she covets the invisible, and is afraid—
and that fear is the commencement of the supernatural,
as Jean de Childra has written.

Pride, ennui, lust and fear are the demon incarnate,
the hallucinated woman sees him and, paraphrasing the
prose of Baudelaire, the Satan of all literatures can say to
the witch intoxicated by joy and terror: "Look at me; I
am the one you do not know, the greatest of all, the only
one that you can love sincerely, poor woman, for I affirm
that you will never, ever know me."

A phantom engendered by desire and a dream, his
strength is in eternal doubt, his charm in suffering, and it
is not in vain that he says to the initiate: "In the infinity
of despair lies the only sensuality; you will weep."

She weeps, and his great power is in her tears; she
weeps and causes weeping, and the pity she inspires soft-
ens courage and will. She has the sensuality of suffering
and she donates its anxiety and its savor to all those who
surround her; she corrupts the chaste by means of pity,
and by means of pity she exasperates the voluptuous and
stimulates them further; avid for the embraces of a god,
since she loves a dream, she refuses herself to amorous
men and her chastity is one lust more, refined, savant
and deleterious. Unsatisfied, in the accursed hours when
the demon escapes her, she dares all sensualities, forgets
her sex and, as a true damned woman, turns to the worst
adventuress with the fatal stigma on the forehead that
troubles men and women. The devil, who has no sex, has
marked her with his seal.

The androgyne! All the malice of the Prince of
Darkness burst forth in the troubled attraction of the

Androgyne, and that imperious charm exerted on both sexes is one of the most revealing characteristics of the witch-woman.

The narcissism that is fundamental to every demoniac, since the devil is only, in sum, the reflection of her own soul, engenders logically the doubly murderous flower of androgyny; and the mathematical adventure of every ensorcelled woman is to die of her own bewitchment; the pagan myth of Narcissus contains everything. That ecstatic agony of an adolescent smitten with his own image is the story of a witch or a sorcerer, perhaps the first sorcerer of all.

That narcissism, an indelible characteristic of demonianism, it was given to me to encounter a few years ago in the works of an artist who, at first, appeared to me to be a pure mystic, and whose works, although less famous, had a strange influence over the literature of the time.

That personal adventure, which is that of many critics, was like the very paraphrase of the text of Satan: "You will weep and you will cause weeping." It is by virtue of pity that the maladroit art, sumptuous and naïve, and also strange, of that even stranger woman, affected souls and took possession of them with an indefinable malaise of tenderness and disappointment. A few lines of Remy de Gourmont, written with the silky green ink of which he has the secret, regarding the work of the artist in question, inspired an unhealthy curiosity in me; there was already a temptation lying in ambush behind the critic's specious phrases:

"A mixture of Catholicism and perversity, her work seems made to illustrate Baudelaire and Barbey d'Aurevilly, and I sense something even more unhealthy there: an exquisite putrefaction that goes as far as to become sumptuous, a charming immorality that is scantly preoccupied with specifying the sexes and leaves androgynous doubt floating like a mist of unhealthy and adorable desires around heads infinitely weary of living, which she details in pastels with a technical science very rare in a woman."

I therefore went to Le Barc de Boutteville,[1] where the paintress was exhibiting; I went and I returned; I took Bourget, Henry Bauer, Henri de Régnier, La Gandara and many others, and I have described elsewhere—or I have attempted to, at least—the disturbance and the profound charm of that deceptive art.[2]

Seven pastels, of a design both expert and naïve, of a deliberate naïvety, going as far as awkwardness, seven monotonous emaciated and unhealthy female heads, always the same, offered in sumptuous and bizarre arrangements—that was the entire exhibition; bathed in I know not what green-tinted luminosity, that surged forth from the high margin of frames, some aureoled like the heads of saints with a halo of incandescent gold, others half-plunged into the gemmed transparency of cups

---

1 The art gallery owned by Louis-Léon Le Barc (1837-1897) was one of the few places where young and *avant garde* artists were able to exhibit in the 1890s; it hosted a series of exhibitions by Impressionists and Symbolists as well as providing Vincent Van Gogh with a Parisian showcase, but it closed when Le Barc died.
2 It is perhaps odd that Lorrain does not name Jeanne Jacquemin, about whom he is very obviously talking, but readers who remembered this article could not have been entirely surprised that she sued him for defamation in 1903 when he extended this strange exercise in psychoanalysis further in "Victime."

and ciboria, like strange cut flowers in a glass, and entitled: *Le Calice; L'Exil; L'Enfant Prodigue, La Fin d'un
jour*; and all those heads were ugly, tortured as they were
by ecstasy and suffering; of a devouring, intoxicated ugliness, and yet disengaging a delectable impression of anguish and pity, which penetrated you. Oh, the forgiving
sadness of those eyes of lapis, the unforgettable mildness
of those tortured heads! The woman of those portraits
was certainly a mystic, but how much more dolorous,
and refined in dolor. She had the cult and the secret of
it; yes, there was Moreau and Odilon Redon in it, but
Gourmont has written elsewhere that it was a much less
pacific Moreau and a more highly mystical Redon. In all
those faces of dream and their weariness of living there
was a kind of joy in suffering; no, they were not cursing
destiny, all those ecstatic or resigned faces, but they were
almost blessing their suffering with all the generosity of
their dolor; those eyes of pardon and those lips of silence
were almost grateful, the memory of the insults and
pain endured was sweet. And a curious psychology was
disengaged therefrom for me, perhaps slightly alarmed;
the author of those pastels had not only the cult but also
the sensuality of dolor; worse, she gave it savor and folly.
"You shall weep and you shall cause weeping."

And from the work I went to the woman, I went to
the household of artists, the man an engraver and the
woman a painter; and I learned the way from the city
to the suburb where they both lived on the edge of the
Seine, smitten with the Primitives and mystical reading,
the atmosphere of which had ended up surrounding
them both like a kind of aura, and by giving them the

ecstatic eyes and luminous foreheads of Gozzoli's arch-angel.[1] The woman especially was extraordinary, with her gaze of a beyond drowned in water, like wings in the intense blue of her irises, the translucent irises of the pitiful severed heads of her pastels, while her mouth, simultaneously sensual and savage, gave her the smile of a mystical bacchante; and that woman had a great charm, and a great trouble also emanated from her, for all her pastels resembled her. She was red-haired and haloed with gold like her fake Botticellis; in her heads, extraor-dinary in their ugliness, she exaggerated the bloodless length of the necks and the dolorous thinness of the faces, but it was her, and nothing but her, in the depths of each frame. She evidently appeared in each of her pas-tels, sought herself there and evoked herself there, and lingered there as if before a mirror. There was certainly in her the amorous ecstasy of Narcissus—what am I saying? there was sadism and worse, sadism turned back against itself, a furious and cold perversity, the solitary sensuality of the maniac laying bare a teasing wound and exciting it with her fingernails, since, in the concentration of those dolorous figures it was herself that she was torturing, crucifying and deforming with so much luxury, refine-ment and leisurely enjoyment.

Oh, those seven visionary pastels, of which one, *Seraphitus*, was devoid of sex while another, *La Fin d'un jour*, was devoid of a body: hallucinating paintings, all marked with the seal of cruelty and androgyny—her

1 Benozzo Gozzoli (c1421-1497) was a pupil of Fra Angelico; the reference is to an image contained in a fresco in the so-called Magi Chapel of the Medici Palace, nowadays adapted as a museum.

"seven sins," as the artist referred to them herself, with a grimace that was almost a smile! Sins of the solitary soul, or pride or lust?

All those who have known and approached that woman will understand me; her maladroit art, almost childish craftsmanship, but of an emotion so sure and so profound, remained an enigma nevertheless for those who do not know; she had painted herself, and that was enough, one might say—but then, what had her life been, and what was her soul?

What were the memories that awoke in her mind with such strange faces: faces of shadow so delectably forgiving and culpable. From what past did they surge forth . . . yes, from what past?

THREE LADIES ON THE ISLAND
(*Le Journal*, 11 June 1896)

IN a summer garden three Ladies are sitting, three
ladies of youth and beauty, all clad in flowery fabrics
with nuances both so soft and pale that the gaze seems
caressed thereby. Their bare feet repose in the grass,
which is thick and mobile, like woven shadow, and
behind them, bright hollyhocks raise their thyrses, in
which silken flowers crumple and deploy, as red as new
wine and as pink as desire.

The tall hollyhocks stand so straight, so bright in
the blue of the August sky that one might think them
church candles burning in broad daylight. On the
horizon, the blue of the sky kisses the blue of the sea,
which is green-tinted; and on the silver-edged shore, the
blue-green of the sea is confounded with the green of
meadows, where pink hawthorns snow, which are belated apple trees, and dwarf apple trees that are precocious
hawthorns. Sheep wander in the meadows, and on the
lapis-lazuli waves the white sail of a galley is rounded out.
But the three Ladies, their backs turned to the landscape,
pay no heed to the flocks scattered like flecks of foam or
the galley with the neck curved like a swan's.

The first is holding a zither in her hand—a small zither in the form of a heart, the strings of which are golden threads—and her blue eyes, the blue of April periwinkles, are languid with melancholy. She is the palest of the three, and over her dress, of the changing green of stormy seas, bouquets of violets are shedding their petals here and there, mingled with iris flowers. Her golden blonde hair flows in streams over her cheeks and circles her temples with a slender band; her blue veil has slid over her frail shoulders, as white as a host, and her bloodless fingers, heavy with jewels, are indolently tormenting the golden strings of the zither while she murmurs fragments of songs in a low voice.

She is Hope.

The second, sheathed in a long dress of silver brocade that makes her resemble a lily, opens two profound eyes very wide, eyes full of shadow, whose gaze burns and dies away like a flame in the rain. A heavy belt studded with rubies grips her flanks so narrowly that it bruises them; and, crowned with blue dune-thistles, of a metallic blue simultaneously hard and gentle, she smiles nevertheless under the ragged foliage that pricks her, and, her entire face ecstatic, she presses to her heart a sheaf of the same blue thistles and branches of holly. A ciborium is at her feet, which shines in the grass, enriched with precious stones, and rubies scintillate in her cup—rubies or blood? The Lady's face is resplendent, all pink, as are her shoulders and her cleavage in her silver dress, but there are two red flowers in the creases of the fabric, where her hands support the thistles and the holly, and sometimes the entire dress becomes pink, while the face, the naked arms and the cleavage whiten and her hair, the color of darkness, suddenly turns red, as red as blood.

She is Fervor.

The third haughty woman, with a delicate profile, a fleshy mouth, mobile nostrils and caressant eyes, is using a golden comb to comb long yellow hair strewn with gems; while she combs her hair she laughs, showing all her teeth, at a polished mirror framed by two vipers. She holds the bright mirror at the height of her lips, and her virgin nudity undulates and quivers through the brilliant and noisy mesh of the tight golden net that serves her as a robe.

Aquamarines, emeralds and opals—an entire florescence of translucent shiny gems—stream over her bare arms, her hollow loins and her thighs, caught in the mesh of the net that clasps them. She has bracelets on her arms, circlets on her ankles and rings on her toes; everything about her is reflective, shiny and radiant, but between her breasts a bouquet of desiccated rises is yellowing, and her laughter rings false, as does the clicking of her scintillating jewels.

She is Illusion.

And Hope, in her green dress, where the flowers are fading, is thinning and paling every day; she is weary of waiting for the one who no longer comes, and of singing songs that no one hears; a mortal sadness invades her blue eyes, and her face slackens from day to day, sagging more heavily under the stream of her hair, paler by the hour.

Her bloodless hands no longer have the strength to torment the golden strings of the zither, not to reattach her transparent veil the color of the sky and water, behind the pleats of which Hope once appeared more desirable to men. She has deceived them for so long and then abandoned all of them in the green meadows of her royal domain; she knows that the immobile galley that has dropped anchor at sea, will never land on her isle, and, dolorous and plaintive, she sings for herself, in a sobbing voice, fragments of songs to which no one any longer listens.

Fervor, in her robe of bloodied snow, indifferent to everything, continues to bruise her breast and temples; her suffering exalts her and her flesh, bewildered by cruel delights, palpitates and weakens with amorous words. What do the galley and its fearful mariners, prudently halted off the isle, matter to her? She hollows out her dolor and nourishes herself thereon; her torture intoxicates her, and, prolonging her agony as she pleases, she loves her torture and drinks her own blood from the ciborium ablaze with gemstones, which enables her to live.

As for Illusion, in her golden sheath, she no longer creates illusions except for herself; centuries have passed since men knew her without ever having seen her. The stories of grandparents have instructed their grandchildren, and from age to age people have transmitted the redoubtable tale of Ulysses and the sirens; she was once called Circe and Calypso, but even the poets amorous of falsehood and fables no longer believe in the kisses of her lips, once so prodigious to humans but today disdained by their children.

Alone on her isle, where no vessel any longer lands, she fools herself before a mirror, infatuated as she is with her vain form; she dazzles her eyes with the gleam of her jewels and intoxicates her ears with their cold clicking.

She is the only one not to see the stain of rust made by the faded roses between her bare breasts, the only one not to sense the sad deathly odor of their desiccated corollas. Anointed with essences and fards, she opens her nostrils to the sea breeze, and like a filly she whinnies noisily at the sea, the turbulent sea from which men come; and, entirely given to her illusion, she combs her yellow hair frantically and deploys it like a flag; and then, twisting it in one hand, lifts it up and agitates it as a signal toward the ships that appear on the horizon, which vanish as soon as they have become visible.

And between two bursts of laughter she proclaims proudly: "I am amour and youth."

And Fervor responds, her pupils dilated, babbling ecstatically: "My wound intoxicates me, I love and I live."

Whereas Hope, bleak, sad and weary, shakes her blonde head and says: "I'm no longer waiting."

And only the innocence of the bleating ewes and lambs wandering on the isle animates the meadows and the boscage and the orchards in flower, to which the men of the present day no longer come.

In a garden on the island three Ladies are sitting, three Ladies of youth and beauty, all clad in flowery fabrics with nuances both so soft and pale that the gaze seems caressed thereby. Their bare feet repose in the grass, which is thick and mobile, like woven shadow, and behind them, bright hollyhocks raise their thyrses, in which silken flowers crumple and deploy, as red as new wine and as pink as desire.

THE GOLD RING
(*Le Journal* 4 December 1897)

What the Missal and the Flowers Said

FAR, far away, very far from here, in the land to which the swallows go when the first frosts of autumn presage winter, there lived a good old king. With his golden crown, his large ermine mantle and his snowy beard, he was the most majestic monarch one could encounter for a thousand leagues around.

His city, the city of a hundred bells, as the ballad says, was also the most curious thing that could be seen. Posed like a saw on the edge of the horizon, on seeing its crenellated ramparts, its harbor full of masts and its marble palaces perforated everywhere by high sculpted gables, turrets with gargoyles and old granite belfries, one might have thought it reminiscent of a vast chessboard forgotten on the shore; it was the marvel of marvels, but the most marvelous thing of all was the palace, an old castle situated a little way outside the city and carved in the very rock of the cliff, so the people said, by the hands of giants and the fays of the sea. It was known as the Spray of

Foam, but instead of being comprised of foam the spray was made of stone, with three terraces and seven towers.

Three crenellated keeps occupied the western part and overhung the waves: the Tower of Seagulls, the Tower of the West Wind and the Tower of Vertigo. Between the latter two an immense stairway descended to the sea: the Giants' Stairway, guarded by a hundred men of marble, the first of which, washed and green-tinted by the tide, seemed to be made of malachite, while those at the top, gilded by the sunset, appeared vermilion.

Such was the palace; it was worth as much as the city and the kingdom on its own, and it overlooked thirty leagues of valleys to the north and twenty leagues of cliffs and the ocean to the west.

The old king lived in the Tower of Seagulls, his hundred and twenty knights in the Tower of the West Wind and Princess Vuilfride, the old king's daughter, languished in retreat in the Tower of Vertigo.

Red-haired, with sharp eyes, so pale that one might have thought her kneaded of snowflakes and sea-spray, she had the touching and unhealthy beauty of pearls devoid of orient, sick turquoises and winter roses.

A tawny blonde with glaucous eyes, the courtiers remembered having seen her as a child with eyes so blue they resembled an April sky and hair so blonde that it was reminiscent of green gold, but in the seven years that she had been living in retreat in the Tower of Vertigo, solitary save for two maidservants, by dint of staring at the cliffs and the waves, the waves had troubled and green-tinted her blue eyes and he sunsets had copper-tinted her blonde tresses. So it was said, at least, but what was not said was that the waves, in taking on the color of her eyes, had taken away her gaze, her soul and her smile.

That smile and that lost gaze the old king and Bishop Afranus had been seeking in vain for seven years; for seven years Princess Vuilfride had not smiled; for seven years her large sea-green eyes had no longer had a gaze.

The clergy called her Vuilfride the Accursed, and the people called her the Bride of the Sea.

The Enchanted Sterlet

Seven years ago, when Princess Vuilfride had been twelve years old, with cornflower blue eyes and golden hair, King Gondoforus—Queen Morfa had been dead for a long time—had the custom of taking his daughter from the hands of her governesses at sunset and going to watch the return of the fishing fleet with the entire court. Leaning over the edge of the terrace that overlooked the sea, the old man and the child watched the fishermen pass along the shore in a troop; and, sometimes descending the Giants' Stairway, King Gondoforus—who was a very good king, popular and greedy—stopped them with a sign at the foot of the stairway, enquiring about their catch and asking to see it. The fish were then heaped up on the steps; a tall black slave gutted them alive, and the king made his choice.

One evening in January, one of those winter evenings when the horizon is entirely red and the sharp breeze announces high winds and cold for the night, one of the fishermen laid out on the slab a monstrous Northern sterlet, so monstrous and magnificent that the old king had never seen its like. There was a uniform cry in the assembled court; the starlet was pink with silver scales, as nacreous as a pearl and so fresh out of the water that it was still breathing.

Princess Vuilfride, very occupied in playing with her dwarf and her two greyhounds, also advanced her pretty blonde head and, very excited by seeing such a beautiful, pink and vibrant fish, asked for it to be put in the guards' pond; but the old king was greedy, and was therefore inexorable; he made a sign to the slave to gut the monster. Then, another cry escaped the crowd; in the entrails of the sterlet, bloody and wide open, shone a jeweled gold ring, so bright and so intensely fiery that one might have thought it forged from a ray of sunlight; the jewel was an aquamarine encased in green gold.

The fisherman took the ring, wiped it on the marble and, bending his knee, offered it to the princess—seeing which, the king, with the majesty of which he was capable, took the ring from his hands, allowed him to kiss his scepter, put the ring on the princess's finger and had the treasurer give a thousand écus to the fisherman. Having acted in that lordly fashion, and having testified before everyone his royal gratitude, the king dismissed him, and four cooks came with a golden tray sustained by three valets to take the starlet away for the royal table.

It appeared that same evening, with all the honors due to the king of sterlets, crowned with parsley, swimming in rose-water, sprinkled with fine gold and laid on a bed of spices and hitherto incomparable shellfish, oysters and pearl-mussels, with red peppers sculpted in coralline branches and marine samphires instead of reeds. The sterlet was found to be excellent and superb, to everyone's taste—especially that of the old king, who ate a third of it on his own.

The Giants' Stairway

Shortly thereafter, Princess Vuilfride fell into a strange melancholy; previously pink, her complexion became etiolated and pale. Neither her black train-bearer nor her white greyhounds interested her any longer; she was visibly pensive, avoiding gazes and seeking solitude, and she remained for hours contemplating the sea.

Some time after that, one night when he was asleep in the Tower of Seagulls, the old king had a dream. In that dream, he saw a marble stairway, the Giants' Stairway, invaded by waves rising in the moonlight, and his daughter lying on the highest step, her eyes closed, asleep—but a bizarre sleep, so profound and so black that it prevented her from feeling and hearing the sea rising around her, and continuing to rise. He—the king, her father—saw her from his tower and tried to wake her; he tried to call out to her but his voice was strangled in his throat; he tried to run, but his tremulous legs collapsed beneath him. That impotence was a true torture. Suddenly, a great cry escaped his lips; the wave breaking at the feet of the princess had brought a great Northern sterlet, and the monster, sliding along her breast, devoured her heart.

The old king awoke bathed in cold sweat.

At the same moment, two fists pounded on his door and the voice of Afranus, the bishop and counselor, cried in the silence: "Open up in the name of Heaven; the life of Princess Vuilfride is ebbing away!"

King Gondoforus had opened the door and, standing on the threshold, was already interrogating him, but Bishop Afranus, without adding anything more, invited him to follow him. The king obeyed; a dull, unaccustomed rumor—the sound of rising water or a human crowd—was murmuring in the tower, and the king was afraid. Torches appeared, setting the darkness ablaze, illuminating scattered white faces, the visors of helmets and the heads of lances. Afranus and the king were on the terrace; the sound was that of the crowd, not of the sea.

At the sight of them, a profound silence fell in all the groups, and as the crowd opened up to give them passage a terrible spectacle awaited the king in the distance on the Giants' Stairway—terrible for a man, horrible for a father.

Pale, her neck extended and her lips quivering, Princess Vuilfride, her eyes hallucinated and staring, disheveled and semi-naked, fixed in a magical stupor, was slowly going down the hundred marble steps that led to the sea; at her feet, around her, the gulf was writhing and roaring in the darkness and the spray, in the sob of the waves and the plaints of the wind. On the horizon there was the eternal battle of the west wind and the moonlit clouds—in sum, all the horror of desolate shores on a winter night at the ocean's edge—but Vuilfride saw nothing and felt nothing. Like the knights, she seemed to be made of marble; fascinated by the abyss, her bare feet were carrying her unconsciously toward the sea; she was following her dream, and the sculpted knights of the stairway were descending in two ranks through the night, to either side of her, escorting her with their shadow and their white specters.

The pale moonlight, the cliffs, the waves, and the sleeping child and the giant knights marching toward the gulf, were not a dream; Princess Vuilfride belonged to the waves and the waves were attracting her; she was under their charm. On her finger was the gold ring with the accursed green stone, shining with a somber gleam, bleak, glaucous and infernal. Motionless, having stopped on the edge of the terrace, Gondoforus watched her descend.

Suddenly, a frisson passed through the assembly; the old king was descending the stairway, the father following his daughter—but the child continued marching, grave and calm, while the king was running down the steps, livid and staggering. He finally reached her on the last step, and, seizing her by the arm, he cried in an abrupt and hoarse voice: "Vuilfride!"

At that cry, the princess, weakening entirely, fell into her father's arms, unconscious.

It was just in time; a wave had just submerged the step, bathing the child and the old man to the knees; at intervals, under the high cliff, the waves repeated to one another the sweet name of Vuilfride, and from one echo to another, they repeated it seven times.

The Ocean was calling.

The old man listened, momentarily stupefied; then, clutching his daughter like a miser, he ran up the steps again, carrying her in his arms.

He only recovered his breath at the top of the stairway, and there, as the ring cast its green-gold reflection into the darkness once again, he tore it from the finger of the princess and advanced to the edge of the terrace.

"Get away, accursed ring!" he said, throwing it over the crenellations. "Fatal gift of Hell, I return you to the abyss."

The Princess with Green Eyes

In the three days that followed, Princess Vuilfride remained unconscious and pale, her eyes closed, in a sleep so similar to death that the king watched over her for the three nights, holding a mirror level with her lips and putting an attentive ear to her heart.

During those three nights, the watchman who kept vigil on the Tower of the West Wind saw the ring shining again on the Giants' Stairway. Like an accursed gaze posted by the waves, it cast its glaucous and green-tinted gleams into the night and darted its radiance toward the Tower of Vertigo, where the princess was asleep. An hour before dawn the ebb tide carried it away; it returned to radiate under the tower for three nights, and then did not return again.

At the third dawn, Vuilfride opened her eyes. The old king was alarmed, and there was alarm among the servants and alarm throughout the palace; the eyes of the princess, once azure blue, had become green: a glaucous and lifeless green, the color of the waves.

The king had returned the aquamarine to the waves, and the waves had returned the aquamarine to the father; it no longer gleamed in the stone of a ring but between two eyelids, mounted in two eyes: his daughter's eyes; the beautiful, vague and troubled eyes no longer had any gaze, nor her lips a smile.

Princess Vuilfride was committed to the abyss, forever languishing, indifferent to everything; she had its frightful emptiness, an emptiness in her eyes and an emptiness in her soul, a void on her lips and in her heart; she had forgotten her name and her prayers, and her eyes, fixed henceforth on the Ocean, had its green transparency and its changing pallor.

HIM!

(*Le Journal*, 17 January 1901)

"AND when I have been to see the boat? With the one from Bône, let us say that they provide objectives for strolling three times a week. The quays, I admit, are enlivened slightly on those days, and all Ajaccio floods there, from the officers of the garrison to the commissionaires of the railway station, to watch the pretty foreigners disembark, who never arrive—for I have been there, and I have not yet encountered in your streets a woman worthy of being followed. What distraction can you offer me?

"It's necessary not to think of excursions; snow holds the mountains, at a height of five hundred meters everything is white, the depths of the gulf are reminiscent of the valley of the Engadine—and to attempt the traditional walk to Salario, above the city, is to risk bronchitis. As for the Punto di Pozzo di Borgo, one starts coughing merely in thinking about it; it is frozen. In other years, a boat service permitted excursions at sea; one could, by traversing the gulf, bathe in the salty air and the sunlight;

the beaches of Isoleila, Porticio and Chiavari on the far side of the bay formed as many havens and ports of call. This winter, the only boat providing the service is under repair in Marseille, and in order to go to Chiavari to visit the Arab penitentiary it requires six hours by carriage— which is to say, departing at dawn and coming back in the evening, in the icy cold of night.

"Oh, the country is very cheerful and I thank you for having made me come. I won't mention the evenings; it's agreed that an invalid ought to go to bed at nine o'clock; but what the devil do you expect me to do with my days? Arrange the employment of my hours for me. You won't see me making visits to the prefect! Can you see me playing tennis with the foreign colony and taking Miss Arabella Smithson, the consumptive young Scotswoman, to the ball, or carrying a racket for Frau Edwige Stopfer, the headmistress of the Swiss school, who apparently flirts with an indigenous coachman and does not disdain fishermen? Terrible, these Oberland glaciers who become volcanoes in their old days. You can no more imagine me swinging my life away in a rocking chair, enveloped by tartan rugs and coiffed in a fur hat, like the worn-out Englishmen and gouty Germans of the hotel. The garden is splendid, I grant you: palms, citrus trees, mimosas and agaves, with a unique panorama, the sea in the background, the city to the left and the cemetery two paces away to the right, but sanitaria are not to my taste and, sunlit as the site is, I shall not fill that hospital garden with my coughing . . . for your hotel is a hospital; the service is first-rate but the corridors reek of creosote and the rooms are embalmed by phenol. Every boarder takes his two Livonian pearls[1] with every meal.

"Oh, doctor, you knew what you were doing in putting me here! You are killing two birds with one stone every time you visit me; I'm a part of your morning round. All that I forgive you, even the insipid nourishment, the eternally boiled meat poorly disguised by brown sauces and the sole desert—walnuts, figs, mandarins and raisins—that I nibble at this hotel. That diet has returned my appetite; I'm dying of hunger and my pangs have enabled me to discover the good Madame Mille, the exquisite and dear Madame Mille, the amiable pastry-cook of the Cours Napoléon, plump, talkative and so agreeable, who makes such succulent blackbird terrines and such tasty citrus compotes. And her myrtle liqueur! To suck it from the teeth and lick it from the lips! I forgive you everything in favor of that fine liqueur, but please, doctor, employ my time, fix me a timetable."

And the doctor, while caressing with a perplexed hand the brilliant brown silk of a well-groomed beard— an entire attitude, or better than an attitude, a poem and a seduction, the long ringed hand of the doctor in the curly and shiny hair of that beard, and what indecision there is in the gesture that smoothes it!—and the doctor, while caressing the perfumed fleece of his chin, says: "We have an unexpected month of January, very unusual, this winter. Can you imagine that it's snowing in Marseille?

---

1 This metaphorical reference to pills should not be confused with modern American "Livonia pills," although Lorrain would doubtless have been amused had he known that such a product would exist one day.

Have you seen the departure of the diligences from the Cours Napoléon every morning at eleven o'clock? Very curious, very picturesque. You see there the true Corsicans, in national costume, in ribbed velvet, with long white beards, the Bellacoscian type that the maquis have worn and all the *cartolina posta* have reproduced, for thirty-two years. I buy a postcard every morning to take to the hotel to send to a little friend in France—the dear creatures believe that I am in danger and shiver delectably."

"The Bellacoscian type does nothing for me. Madame Mille has told me that they are thus costumed at the Prefecture to comply with the tastes of winter visitors. I have not, therefore, gone to watch your diligences depart; I am familiar with those of Algeria, which are constructed on the same model . . . yours are even more uncomfortable and even smaller, with their panels painted green and dark red; one might think them a batch of *camerera mayor* to see all those travelers in mourning. And to think that Bonaparte took one of those carriages to go to Bastia via Vizzavona and Corte when he departed for Brienne! I know the couplet . . . There's also the pilgrimage to the Maison Bonaparte and the visit to the museum with souvenirs of Napoléon, but I don't have the soul of Jean de Milly every day. England took the eagle and Austria the eaglet.

"The success of Monsieur Rostand has left us—continentals, that is—a little blasé with regard to the epic of the historic giant. I'm astonished that you haven't yet proposed that I go to the railway station to watch trains arrive: the mountain-dwellers in vendetta, rifles on their shoulders, commencing to fire their weapons as soon as they are on the platform; the carrying of blunderbusses being prohibited in the city, those little local formalities sometimes organize the gunfire of interested platoons between two trains—but what do you expect? All of that leaves me cold; I've traveled the world too much; my memories of Sicily defend me against Corsica, and the picturesque finds me recalcitrant.

"Good! Now the sun in quitting us! Adieu, light of Africa: look at the melancholy of the bay in that mist: the entire landscape is a sad blue attenuated by slate-gray. Are those leaden mountains sufficiently exiled?"

The heartbroken doctor said nothing more; his nose over his plate, he ate, meekly resigned to my complaints and to the hotel menu. We were finishing lunch in the light, filtered by blinds, of a long glazed gallery, having taken refuge there in prudent fear of the table d'hôte; we were, in any case, the last to remain at table, the other diners having already spread out in the garden, basking in the sunlight in a congestion of the plaids, shawls and cloaks that only English people and Germans parade through the world: phthitics from beyond the Rhine and splenetics from beyond the Manche rubbing shoulders in the slender blue shadow of the palm trees. The golden balls of mimosas and the bloody thyrses of red-flowering cacti prepared the décor of the soft azure of the mountains and the gulf: attenuated melancholy, the muffled charm of a landscape for consumptives and globe-totters, extenuated by civilization, run aground in a haven of exile and somnolent agony between the olive groves, the green oaks and the sea.

At that moment, the sun reappeared, making the snow on the peaks and the displayed gulf sparkle, cruelly accentuating the bile and chlorosis of complexions, and the lassitude of eyes and smiles by the same token, as well as the exhausted slackness of faces. The women strolling in the garden seemed flabby and worn out, like as many fatigued handbags.

What was I doing in that garage of ancient objects of travel? I felt a muted tide of rancor against the doctor rising within me, a wind of injustice lifted me up, and an awkward silence began to weigh upon us.

Suddenly, the glazed door of the dining room opened wide, and, gigantic, with his sturdy frame, his bulbous stomach and his heavy face with sagging jowls, *He* appeared—for it was *Him*, there was no mistaking it: they were his large bulging eyes and heavy eyelids, it was his regular profile, his thick lips and his stout chin—a face from a medallion of the Roman decadence, redeemed by the grace of the smile and the grandiose beauty of the gaze; for He also had limpid and pensive eyes, a slow gait, and even a rare flower in his buttonhole. It was Him, but rejuvenated by twenty years, Him in all the splendor of his triumphs as a poet and an author, Him, pampered, adulated and courted, disputed in offers of dollars by London and New York; and as I knew that he was dead, in what misery and what abandonment, the double mystery of the portrait of Dorian Gray imposed itself imperiously on my memory; I risked the impoliteness of turning round abruptly in my chair in order to follow the alarming resemblance for longer with my eyes. It was striking; a twin could not have been more identical.

An elegant young woman with smooth blonde hair, and long sturdy feet clad in flat shoes, accompanied the false Oscar, like a companion of the English Cook Agency.

"The portrait of Dorian Gray," my doctor thought aloud—we had thought it simultaneously. "One could believe him a ghost, couldn't one? What a story of the afterlife one could base on that resemblance—a goblin tale, as they say in London, a fine subject for a Christmas story.[1] If I had encountered that Englishman aboard ship on the night of the thirty-first of December I would have thought it a sign. Can you imagine that false Oscar suddenly appearing, at night, on the deck of a steamer in a choppy and sinister sea . . . ?

"Brrr, a day of the dead in denial. It's an accident of race; strange analogies can flourish then. In any case, the fatal resemblance must be very embarrassing for that Englishman. Yes, one might believe him resuscitated. Do you know that you keep your promises poorly, man of scant word as you are. The story of Christ and Lazarus of that poor Wilde, which you have announced, and sounded its trumpet, you still owe to us, you know."

"So be it; I'll give it to you, then, for it's full of melancholy, and will fit well into the frame of this gulf and this

---

1 In fact, an English reader of the time would probably have referred to the burgeoning tradition of "Christmas ghost stories," but Lorrain might have been aware of the existence of James Bowker's *Goblin Tales of Lancashire* (1878) and probably knew that the first story in which Charles Dickens had laid the foundations for the tradition of Christmas tales of the supernatural was "The Story of the Goblins who Stole a Sexton" in *The Pickwick Papers* (1836), published some years before his famous sequence of Christmas Books begun with *A Christmas Carol* (1843).

décor of winter sunlight. But I won't tell it to you with the deliberate slowness of his modulated and precious diction, nor the deliberate emphasis of his gesture. In any case, it has a slight variation of the text in the Gospel.

"So, Lazarus was dead, descended into the tomb, and Marthe, having come to meet Jesus on the road to Bethany, said to him, weeping: 'Lord, if you had been here, my brother would not be dead!'

"Once they had arrived in the house of the two sisters, Mary threw herself at Jesus' feet and also said to him: 'Lord, if you had been here, my brother would not be dead!'

"And Jesus, seeing that she was weeping, and that the Jews who had come with her were also weeping, shivered mentally and was troubled himself. Then he said: 'Where have you put him?' and they replied: 'Come and see, Lord.'

"Then Jesus wept and the Jews said to one another: 'See how he loved him.' But there were some who said: 'Could you not have prevented him from dying?' And Jesus, trembling, went to the tomb. It was a grotto and it was sealed by a stone that had been placed there.

"Jesus said: 'Take away that stone.'

"Marthe, the sister of the dead man, then said: 'Lord, he already smells bad, for he has been dead for four days.' But Jesus replied: 'Have I not promised you that if you have faith, you will see the glory of God?'

"So they removed the stone and Jesus, raising his eyes to Heaven, set about praying, and then, having prayed, he approached the grotto and cried in a loud voice: 'Lazarus, come forth!'

"And suddenly, the man who was dead got up, with his hands and feet bound with bandages and his face enveloped by a cloth, and Jesus said to them: 'Unbind him and let him walk.'

"But—here commences the poet's variant—the resuscitated Lazarus remained sad; instead of falling at the feet of Jesus, he stood apart with an air of reproach, and, Jesus having advanced toward him, he said: 'Why have you lied to me? Why are you still lying in talking to them about Heaven and the glory of God? There is nothing in death, nothing at all, and the man who is dead is really dead; I know that, having come back from out there!'

"And Jesus, with a finger over his mouth, gazing at Lazarus imploringly, replied: 'I know that; don't tell them!'"

A PARTIAL LIST OF SNUGGLY BOOKS

G. ALBERT AURIER *Elsewhere and Other Stories*
CHARLES BARBARA *My Lunatic Asylum*
S. HENRY BERTHOUD *Misanthropic Tales*
LÉON BLOY *The Desperate Man*
LÉON BLOY *The Tarantulas' Parlor and Other Unkind Tales*
ÉLÉMIR BOURGES *The Twilight of the Gods*
CYRIEL BUYSSE *The Aunts*
JAMES CHAMPAGNE *Harlem Smoke*
FÉLICIEN CHAMPSAUR *The Latin Orgy*
BRENDAN CONNELL *Unofficial History of Pi Wei*
BRENDAN CONNELL *The Metapheromenoi*
RAFAELA CONTRERAS *The Turquoise Ring and Other Stories*
ADOLFO COUVE *When I Think of My Missing Head*
QUENTIN S. CRISP *Aiaigasa*
LADY DILKE *The Outcast Spirit and Other Stories*
CATHERINE DOUSTEYSSIER-KHOZE
   The Beauty of the Death Cap
ÉDOUARD DUJARDIN *Hauntings*
BERIT ELLINGSEN *Now We Can See the Moon*
ERCKMANN-CHATRIAN *A Malediction*
ALPHONSE ESQUIROS *The Enchanted Castle*
ENRIQUE GÓMEZ CARRILLO *Sentimental Stories*
EDMOND AND JULES DE GONCOURT *Manette Salomon*
REMY DE GOURMONT *From a Faraway Land*
REMY DE GOURMONT *Morose Vignettes*
GUIDO GOZZANO *Alcina and Other Stories*
GUSTAVE GUICHES *The Modesty of Sodom*
EDWARD HERON-ALLEN *The Complete Shorter Fiction*
EDWARD HERON-ALLEN *Three Ghost-Written Novels*
RHYS HUGHES *Cloud Farming in Wales*
J.-K. HUYSMANS *The Crowds of Lourdes*
J.-K. HUYSMANS *Knapsacks*
COLIN INSOLE *Valerie and Other Stories*
JUSTIN ISIS *Pleasant Tales II*